D1521685

DEADLY BREW
Copyright © 2017 by Karen MacInerney

Printed in the USA.

Cover Design and Interior Format
© KILLION
THE
GROUP, INC.

A DEWBERRY FARM

Deadly Brew

MYSTERY

Karen MacInerney

NATIONAL BESTSELLING AUTHOR

Books in the Dewberry Farm Mystery Series

Killer Jam

Fatal Frost

Deadly Brew

Book 4, Title Forthcoming (Fall 2018)

Dedicated to Dorothy MacInerney, a talented author, grandmother extraordinaire, and the best mother-in-law in the world.

I love you!

Chapter 1

OCTOBER IN TEXAS, UNFORTUNATELY, ISN'T a lot different from July in Texas—at least weather-wise. If you work in downtown Houston, it just means you keep the AC turned on, but it can be problematic if you live in Buttercup, Texas, and you're trying to keep two cows, three goats, a flock of chickens, a small peach orchard and several fields of vegetables alive in 100-degree heat with no rain.

I looked out from my kitchen table at the cloudless sky, and began to fret again as my eyes dropped to the rows of wilting broccoli starts I'd put out two weeks ago. I was watering them twice a day, and they were still struggling; we'd had almost no rain for months. With the grass in the pastures bleached and dead, I was having to pay more than I'd budgeted to feed the goats and the cows, and my already-small bank account was rapidly dwindling. It was a good thing I had a well, I thought, as I pushed away from the line of figures I'd been writing out and headed out to move the hoses. If I had a water bill, it would sink me.

I'd bought Dewberry Farm, which belonged to my grandmother when I was growing up, almost two years ago, and had been slowly bringing it back to life. I loved the yellow farmhouse, the rolling hills carpeted with bluebonnets in the spring, and the slow, friendly pace of life in Buttercup. I'd taken a big risk when I quit my job as a reporter in Houston and put my life savings into the farm. There had been ups and downs, but I'd really come to treasure the rhythm of life in the country. I took great satisfaction in eating cheese I'd made myself, in growing my own vegetables, in bringing life back to the farmstead I'd known as a girl. And it was wonderful being part of a small community.

I just hoped I'd be able to keep things going.

"I'll come see you in a minute!" I called to the goats, who had spotted me and were over at the edge of the fence. Hot Lips, as usual, was chewing on the wire, while her daughter, Carrot, stood at her side. Gidget and her daughter, Priscilla, were pushing their noses through the fence and bleating. My Jersey cow, Blossom, and her daughter, Peony, were eyeing me with interest, too. It was turning into quite a farm family, I thought with satisfaction.

I scanned the tomato plants—I'd planted them in September, hoping for a fall crop—and was chagrined to see yellow, curling leaves on a few of them. When I looked closer, I spotted a few spider mites.

Drat.

I preferred to water tomato plants from below—water can spread viruses—but spider mites hate humidity and can be washed off leaves, so I decided to give it a shot. I grabbed the hose and prepared to give the leaves a dousing. As I pulled the trigger on the hose end, there were a few convulsive sprays of water and then the stream reduced to a trickle.

I searched the hose back to the faucet, looking for a kink, but there was none. Was there something wrong with the faucet? Turning the handle did nothing. I detached the hose and walked over to the house to attach it to the hose bib by the kitchen. When I turned the faucet on, though, the same thing happened.

My stomach twisted into a knot as I spun the handle again and again.

Either there was a problem with my pump, or something much, much worse had happened.

My well had run dry.

"You want the bad news, or the good news?" asked Lenny Froehlich when he walked out of the well house.

"Bad news first," I said.

"Well's run dry," he told me, his mouth sliding into a grimace.

"Please tell me the good news is better," I said.

"Good news is, if you go deeper, you should be okay," he said.

"And how much will that cost?" I asked.

"Depends," he said. "Shouldn't be that expensive, though."

"No?" I asked, feeling hopeful.

"Only a couple of thousand," he said. "I can't get out for a few weeks, though; wells going dry all over town."

"A few weeks?" I asked. "How am I supposed to water things until then?"

"Truck it in," he suggested.

"And how much does that cost?" I asked, not wanting to know.

He shrugged. "Have to talk to the county, I guess. I don't know the going rate."

That's helpful, I thought, glancing up at the sky. Still

cloudless. "What do I do in the meantime?" I asked.

"Fill up some jugs at a neighbor's and see if you can keep things going," he suggested. "And pray for rain."

"Don't worry about it now," my best friend, Quinn Sloane, said when I called her. She owned the Blue Onion café on the square in town; I often came and helped her out to supplement my income. "I'll call around; we'll figure out a way to get you through until you get it going again. It probably won't be until tomorrow, though. Do the animals have enough water to make it until then?"

"They do."

"Well, stop worrying about it for now and go get gussied up for the Witches' Ball. It's good timing; people look out for each other here, and when they find out you're in a bind, maybe someone can help you figure something out."

With all the well issues, I'd forgotten about the Witches' Ball, which had created quite a stir in Buttercup. "I'm not exactly in the partying mood," I said, surveying my limp broccoli plants and fretting. "It's like playing the violin while Rome burns."

"That's the thing about farming," she said. "You gotta let go of what you can't control. Now, go put on your hat and I'll be there to pick you up in ten minutes."

I hung up the phone and reached down to pat Chuck, my bald rescue poodle, who was much more concerned with whether I was going to slip him a piece of bacon than whether the well would miraculously recover. I'd managed to fill a gallon jug with water for him; I checked his water dish, gave him a kiss on the head, and headed into my bedroom to change.

I surveyed myself in the mirror. The sun had browned my cheeks and nose, and my hair had streaks I hadn't seen before. I was fitter than I'd been when I moved to the farm eighteen months ago, with biceps I hadn't known existed and new calluses on my hands. It felt good to use my body every day, and although I could read the worry in my eyes, I looked healthy. I pulled my hair back at the nape of my neck, swiped on a bit of mascara and lipstick—Tobias, the gorgeous vet I'd been dating, would be at the ball, after all—and shrugged into the long black dress I had picked up at Goodwill with Quinn. I tossed a belt around my waist and slipped into some pointy-toe boots, then added a crooked black hat.

If nothing else, I told myself as I adjusted the brim over my eyes, at least I'd get to see Tobias tonight. Which made me decide to add a little eyeliner.

I finished dressing and went to the back room to check on the goat soap I'd made a few weeks before; it was curing nicely. I'd been hoping to get some bees and harvest my own honey and beeswax, but if I needed to spend money on the well...

I pushed the thought aside and put some kibble in Chuck's bowl. One thing at a time, Lucy. One thing at a time.

Twenty minutes later, I was in the backseat of Quinn's truck, heading to the first-ever Buttercup Witches' Ball. Quinn's red, curly hair had been sprayed with glitter, and she was dressed in a sparkly dress she'd picked up on the same shopping trip; she was attending as Glinda the Good Witch. Flora Kocurek sat in the front seat; I'd forgotten we'd offered to have her join us. Her only concession to the theme was a purple sweatshirt with a pumpkin in a witch's hat appliquéd to the front of it. It hung loose on her bony frame.

I surveyed the crowd as we pulled into the car-filled grassy field next to the Honeyed Moon Mead Winery. Despite the tongues wagging around town—a Witches' Ball, run by an actual Wiccan!—it appeared the whole town of Buttercup had gotten over any qualms about the winery's Halloween party. After all, the proceeds went toward the animal rescue organization the winery's owner ran on her property.

"I think the whole town showed up," Flora said.

"Molly's going to be sad she missed it," I said. My friend Molly Kramer was out of town for her sister's birthday party, and wouldn't be back until close to Halloween.

"I love the decorations!" Quinn said. "It really does look magical!"

I had to admit she was right. The Alexandre sisters had done it up right. The two had moved from New Orleans not long ago and set about turning an old farm into their dream business, the Honeyed Moon Mead Winery. Flickering lanterns had been strung up in the branches of spreading live oaks around a central clearing, which was ringed by tables filled with all kinds of ghoulish goodies. A wall of jack-o'-lanterns glowed near the entrance, and I could see several costumed people gathered around a steaming cauldron.

"You think that's mead in the cauldron, or cider?" I asked.

"I'm kind of hoping it's mead," Quinn said. "I don't know how she got it to steam like that, though." What appeared to be smoke poured over the rim of the cauldron and Serafine was ladling out cups of something and handing them to partygoers. "Have you tried Serafine's Moon Mead?"

"Yes... it's addictive. Like liquid flowers, only with a touch of spice. I picked up a bottle last week when I was talking to Serafine about starting a hive of my own," I said. "It was a splurge, but I couldn't resist."

"You're adding bees to Dewberry Farm?" Flora asked.

I shrugged. "Why not? Assuming everything doesn't shrivel from drought, that is."

"I'm sure it'll rain soon," Quinn reassured me.

"Anyway, assuming I survive the coming winter, I plan to start a hive in the spring. I've got cows, goats, and chickens already. They don't take up too much room."

Flora sucked in her breath. "I hope you're not allergic! My aunt got stung once; she ended up in the hospital with anaphylactic shock."

I glanced at Flora in the rearview mirror. "That sounds horrible. I hope she made it through!"

"She did, but she blew up like a balloon. Almost died. I hope there aren't any bees out tonight; if it's genetic, I could be allergic, too."

"The hives are well away from the main area," Quinn said. "Besides, it'll be dark soon... and with the cold snap, they're probably all tucked up keeping warm anyway."

"Here's hoping," Flora said ominously, and Quinn and I exchanged glances. We'd taken Flora with us because we were trying to help her mingle with the community; since the loss of her mother, she'd become something of a hermit.

"It's too bad Mama didn't make it. She'd have been a natural here," Flora said as I pulled into a grassy spot not too far from the main goings-on. Although she'd loved her mother, she was still bitter.

"She wasn't all bad," Quinn protested, although Flora's mother, Nettie, had never been particularly popular with either of us. The fact that she'd sold me Dewberry Farm and then turned around and tried to plant an oil well in my broccoli patch hadn't helped.

"You didn't live with her for half a century," Flora objected. "I loved her, but she had her faults. Speaking of faults, look who else dropped in."

"Oh, boy," Quinn said, following her pointing finger to where Bug Wharton and his brother, Mitch, were clambering out of his enormous extended king cab Dodge Ram.

"There's enough chrome on that thing you can see it from space," I said, shielding my eyes as he slammed the door. The sun was setting, and the flash off the grille just about blinded me. "How much do you think that thing cost?"

Quinn flipped down the mirror and inspected her sparkly hair. "More than your farm, most likely. Peter can't stand him."

I glanced at my friend. "He's the one who started the exotic game ranch just down the road from Peter's place, isn't he?"

"Exactly." She flipped the mirror shut and grimaced. "It's one of those terrible places where they raise endangered animals and sell the right to shoot them."

I knew exotic game ranches were big business in Texas, and I'd occasionally driven past a high-fenced pasture with animals I'd only seen on nature specials and in zoos grazing behind the fence, but it was strange to think of one in Buttercup. "It sounds pretty awful."

"Some people argue they're kind of like living arks... that they're saving endangered species," Flora piped up from the backseat. "Mother thought about starting one, actually."

"With all due respect to your mother, it sounds pretty heartless," I said.

Quinn flipped the mirror open again and wiped a bit of sparkle from her forehead. "Too much glitter, do you think?"

"It's Halloween," I said. "Is there such a thing as too much glitter?"

She glanced at me. "I guess you're right. Looks like Peter's already here," she said, pointing to a van with a verdant scene and "Green Haven Farm" painted on it. It was Buttercup's only fry-oil-powered vehicle, and belonged to Quinn's beau, local organic farmer Peter Swenson. Peter and Quinn had been seeing each other for several months, and were so happy I would have been jealous if I hadn't been seeing the handsome local vet, Tobias Brandt. Quinn glanced back up at the mirror and adjusted her hair; I could see a smile of anticipation on her glossed lips. "Ready?"

"I am," I said, wondering when Tobias would arrive. My veterinarian boyfriend had had an urgent call out near La Grange; he said he'd get here as soon as he could. He was a frequent visitor at Honeyed Moon Mead Winery.

The owner, Serafine, asked, "What's Peter going as, anyway?"

"I think the Grim Reaper," she said as we walked through the pasture toward the wall of flickering jack-o'-lanterns. "He found a scythe in the barn, and he had some old burlap he was planning to dye black."

"The Grim Reaper and Glinda the Good Witch. Quite a combo," I said, grinning.

"I'm hoping to find a Grim Reaper of my own," Flora said, adjusting her sweatshirt.

"I hope so too," I said.

"I've got a date in La Grange this week," she admitted, blushing.

"Good for you!" Quinn said.

"I'm just afraid I'll make the same mistake again," Flora said. Her last boyfriend—fiancé, actually—had turned out to be something of a bad egg.

"I know what to watch for," Quinn said. "You can talk to me about red flags."

"Oh, that's right... your ex," Flora said with a shiver. Jed Stadtler, Quinn's ex, had a history of assaulting my friend, and was, thankfully, spending some quality time behind bars for his offenses. "We don't have very good taste in men, do we?" Flora said with a sad smile.

"Fortunately, that's changing," I said, spotting Peter, who was wearing a long black cloak and carrying a scythe. "Maybe your guy in La Grange will turn out to be a Prince Charming."

"I'd settle for a Grim Reaper," Flora replied, looking at Peter. "So would Serafine's sister Aimee, from what I hear. Look... there she is now."

Sure enough, Aimee's braids had been tucked up into a sparkly headdress, and her dark, almond-shaped eyes were accentuated with heavy eyeliner. Her coffee-colored skin glowed in the low light from the candles; she looked exotic and mysterious. Which was appropriate, since she'd set up a booth with tarot cards not far from the steaming cauldron. As we approached, she walked over and tugged on Peter's black sleeve, enticing him for a reading. Reluctantly, he let her drag him over to her booth and arrange him in a chair across from her.

"I hate to spoil her moment," Quinn said as Aimee handed him the big cards to shuffle.

We hung back as he gave them a perfunctory shuffle and set them on the table.

"What's your question?" Aimee asked in a husky, seductive voice, leaning forward and fixing him with a penetrating gaze.

"She is pretty gorgeous," Quinn murmured to me, biting her lip. "Should I be worried?"

"I think you're fine," I reassured her in a low voice.

"Question?" Peter told Aimee, looking uncomfortable. "I don't really have one."

"Nothing about romance?" she asked, fluttering mascaraed lashes.

"Subtle," Quinn whispered to me.

"Ah, no," Peter said, glancing around as if he'd rather be anywhere else. Unfortunately for him, he inadvertently caught the eye of Teena Marburger, who also had a crush on him.

"We'll just do a general reading, then," Aimee told him, looking disappointed.

As she smoothed out the tablecloth, Teena tottered over on tall, high-heeled silver shoes. "Peter!" she called, her eyes shining. She was dressed in striped stockings and a short, form-fitting black dress, and looked much older—and sexier—than a high-school senior.

"Oh, hi," Peter said weakly.

"Poor guy," I said.

"I'm going in," Quinn announced, striding over to claim her man.

As she touched his shoulder, he jumped; then, when he turned and recognized Quinn, his face broke into a smile of relief. Aimee and Teena, on the other hand, looked as if they had just sucked on lemons.

"Quinn! You look great!'

She smiled back at him. "Thanks. You look... menacing," she replied, pointing to the scythe.

"Aimee was just about to do a reading for me," he said, looking back at the card reader. "You've met Quinn, right?"

"We've met at the café," Aimee said coolly.

"Hi, Aimee. Hi, Teena." Quinn nodded to the two women as Flora and I joined the group around the table.

"I don't usually have quite such an audience for a reading," Aimee said, looking uncomfortable.

"I'm curious to see how it works," Teena volunteered. "I sometimes... well, I know things, but I've never done anything with tarot cards before."

"If you like, maybe I can teach you sometime," Aimee offered, softening a bit. She looked at Peter. "Sure you don't have a question?"

"Well, maybe I do. Think the cards can tell me what to do about that exotic game ranch?"

"You want to know what's going to happen with the game ranch?"

"Sure," he said with a shrug of his cloaked shoulder. "Why not?"

As we watched, she plucked the top card from the stack and laid it down on the cloth.

"The first card is the situation card, in this case, the king of pentacles," she intoned, laying down a card picturing a man on a throne, clutching what looked like a gold coin. "A man with dark hair, who is a master of money."

"Sounds like Bug," Peter quipped.

"Only not so much hair these days," Quinn added,

one hand lying proprietarily on her man's shoulder.

"The second card," Aimee continued, "is what crosses you." She laid down a card with more of the gold coins, only this one was a man clutching at them. "Greed," she said.

"That's about right."

As we watched, she put down the rest of the cards. I didn't know how much she interpreted based on what she knew of the situation and how much was the cards, but she did do a pretty accurate job of describing the situation. A dark-haired man doing something for money that wasn't popular or ethical, which we kind of already knew. The cards didn't say much about what to do, though—at least not that I could see.

"And finally," she announced, "the outcome card." She laid down the last card with a flourish, and Teena sucked in her breath. It showed a man dressed very much like Peter—the Grim Reaper—carrying a scythe and riding a pale horse.

"The death card!" Teena murmured.

"Death doesn't always mean actual death," Aimee corrected her. "It often means change, the erasing of something old to make room for the new."

"But it doesn't," Teena said, her eyes looking unfocused. "This is an omen."

Quinn and I exchanged looks; we'd learned to trust Teena's hunches. "What do you mean?" Quinn asked.

"Someone's going to die," she said, and goose bumps crawled up my arms.

Chapter 2

"NONSENSE," AIMEE SAID, SWEEPING THE cards off the table. "It just means change. Things as they are are going to be reshuffled, and there will be something new."

"Like an expanded exotic game ranch?" Peter asked.

She shrugged. "It's hard to say," she said. "Maybe something we haven't even considered will come to pass. That will be twenty dollars," she added.

"What?" Peter protested. "I thought it was free!"

"I'll discount it because I like you," Aimee said, giving him a seductive half smile. "It all goes to the animal rescue operation, anyway."

"In that case, take twenty," Peter the Reaper said, reaching under his robes for his wallet and fishing out a twenty-dollar bill.

Teena's eyes were full of warning. "Be careful, Peter," she said.

"What do you mean?" he asked.

"I just... I just have a feeling. Something to do with bees."

"We are at a mead winery," Aimee pointed out.

"Are you allergic to bees?" Quinn asked Peter.

"No," he said, and turned to Teena with a kind smile. "But thank you... I'll keep an eye out for swarms."

She nodded and turned away after darting a glance

at Quinn.

"Poor girl," Quinn murmured as she fled. "I really hope she finds someone to date; she's so beautiful and kind."

"She will," Peter said. "And hopefully, he'll be closer to her age. Let's go get a drink," he suggested, and together we walked over toward the bubbling cauldron in the middle of the clearing. "Have any of you eaten anything yet?"

"No," I admitted.

"The food's great; I had some corn a few minutes ago, and there's sausage on a stick over in the corner there. The sausage's from Elgin—it's delicious."

"I can't believe so many people turned out," I said. "After all the controversy and everything."

"Oh, there are still a few grumblers," Peter said as we approached the cauldron, which was suspended over a bed of glowing coals. The contents were definitely mead; I could smell the spicy, honeyed scent perfuming the air. "But they're all enjoying the mead."

As he spoke, there was the sound of angry voices coming from near the cauldron.

Serafine stood with her arms crossed, looking every bit the magical figure. Her black braids were swept up on top of her head, and she wore a long, star-spangled gown with a black velvet cloak. The expression on her face made her look like she'd just found a toad in her cauldron. Across from her was Bug Wharton, his face bright purple, looking like he was about to blow a gasket. His brother, Mitch, hovered between them, looking nervous.

"You're a cruel, evil man," Serafine shouted. "Those animals… you're raising them by hand and selling their lives to the highest bidder, all so you can line your pockets."

"It's business," he said. "And it's legal, and there's nothing you can do about it. Why don't you and your pagan friends find some other town to pollute with your demonic rituals?"

"We were here first," she announced. "And I'll fight you with everything I have at my disposal," she said.

"I just want something to drink, not a lecture," he said. "Here. Go ahead and save your animals. I'll do what I want with mine." He tossed a twenty on the table next to Serafine. "Keep the change."

Her tilted eyes narrowed as she handed him a cup. "Drink deep," she said. "And remember, what you put into the world comes back to you thrice over."

It sounded like an incantation as much as a challenge. Bug didn't look away as he took the cup, drained it, and threw it on the ground, crushing it with his heel. "Overrated," he said, and turned away, swaggering over to the sausage stand as the onlookers watched with bated breath. Mitch, looking uncomfortable, trailed behind him.

Serafine bent down to retrieve the paper cup and tossed it onto the coals beneath the cauldron, where it flared quickly. Then she brushed her hands off, as if ridding herself of something unpleasant, and turned to the next person in line.

"So, he's going ahead with the exotic ranch plan?" Peter asked, anger in his voice. He clenched the scythe hard.

"It's already a done deal, I'm afraid," I said.

"It's so frustrating. I talked to the mayor, but she said there was nothing she could do," Peter told me. "So did Serafine." As he said her name, she looked up and saw us, and her face broke into a smile. "Lucy! You made it!

And Peter and Quinn, too."

"And Flora," I added as we walked over to where she stood, indicating our sweatshirted companion.

"Nice to meet you, Flora," Serafine said, reaching out to shake the woman's hand. "Can I get you some mead?" she asked.

"We'd love some," I said as she ladled up a few more cups.

"I can't believe that man showed up here," Serafine said, glancing at the twenty on the table. "I didn't want to take his money, but the animals need everything they can get. Food and litter are expensive."

"No luck with the mayor on keeping the ranch from going ahead?" Peter asked

She shook her head as she handed him a cup. "I can file a complaint, but I can't find a way to stop it. I don't understand why he's doing it," she said. "From what I hear, he's already got loads of money. Although I don't know how; last I heard, he's working part-time down at the courthouse."

"I'll talk to the mayor, too," Flora volunteered.

"Thanks," Serafine said. "I don't know if it will do anything, but every little bit helps." She turned to me. "Given any more thought to having a hive of your own?" she asked.

"I'm thinking I'm going to give it a shot," I said. "Just tell me what to do."

"Great," she said, grinning, then turned to Tobias, who had walked up while we were talking. "I hope you don't mind, by the way... one of my rescues isn't looking so hot. Would you mind checking on her while you're here?"

"Sure," he said, leaning over to give me a kiss on the head in greeting. "I'm really thankful for what you're doing."

She was about to respond when someone yelled "Help!" from near the sausage stand. It was Bug Wharton's brother, Mitch.

"What's wrong?"

"It's Bug," Mitch said. "In his truck... he's in trouble. Hurry!"

Tobias dropped his cup and rushed after Mitch as he turned and raced to Bug's enormous pick-up truck. Peter, Quinn and I followed.

Mitch was right; Bug was in trouble. The truck door was open, and Bug was sprawled across the driver's seat. His face had swelled up, and his lungs whistled as he struggled to breathe.

"EpiPen," Bug said in a strangled voice. "Glove compartment."

"I've got it," Peter said, racing to the passenger side and throwing open the door.

As Tobias unbuttoned Bug's collar, I pulled out my phone and dialed 911. What seemed like an eternity later, Peter dug the syringe out of the glove compartment and handed it to Tobias.

As we watched, Tobias plunged the needle into Bug's thigh. "This should work pretty fast," he said. Relief flooded me, and not for the first time, I was thankful for Tobias's medical training. I didn't like Bug, but that didn't mean I wanted him to die

Unfortunately, as we watched, his breath whistled in and out a few more times and then stopped completely.

By the time the paramedics arrived, Tobias had been giving Bug CPR for fifteen minutes, but there was still

no sign of a heartbeat.

"I don't understand it," Tobias said, shaking his head as he stepped back and let the paramedics take over. His eyes looked haunted; I could tell he felt personally responsible for what had happened. "We got him the EpiPen so fast."

"Maybe it wasn't an allergic reaction," I suggested.

"It had the hallmarks of one, though," Tobias said. "No sign of blockage in his throat. And he asked for the EpiPen." He turned to Bug's brother. "Did he have any allergies you know of?"

"Bees," he said.

"Could it have been the honey in the mead?" I asked, thinking of the cup he'd drained.

Tobias shook his head. "Highly unlikely. It's the venom that causes the allergy, not the honey."

"I didn't see any bees," I said. "Plus, it's getting dark; they usually aren't out now."

"There's one there," Peter pointed out. He was right; there was a small, lifeless black and gold body in a crumpled cone of paper in the front seat.

"There was one in the cab when we got here," Peter said. "It flew out when I opened the door." He reached for the cone of paper.

"Don't touch it," I warned him. "It could be evidence."

Mitch Wharton blinked, and I took a look at him for the first time. He looked like his brother, but scaled down, somehow. His chin was a little less strong, and although he and his brother shared a barrel chest and six-feet-plus in height, somehow Mitch seemed less of a presence. Like a cup of tea from the second steeping. "Evidence?" he asked. "Of what?"

As Tobias and I exchanged looks, a siren blared next

to us, announcing that Sheriff Rooster Kocurek was on the scene.

"Thank goodness we have the professionals involved," Quinn said dryly.

"What's goin' on here?" Rooster crowed as he heaved himself out of his Crown Victoria, his reddish wattle wobbling over his too-tight polyester collar.

"This man stuck my brother in the leg with an EpiPen and he died," Mitch volunteered.

"It looked like an allergic reaction," Tobias said. "He asked for the EpiPen."

"And you're the one who told me where it was," Peter pointed out.

"It looks like someone might have put some bees in the truck," I said, pointing to the cone of paper on the front seat.

Rooster squinted at the dead bee on the paper, and then at me. "I'll talk to you all separately in a minute," he said, in a typically imperious manner, and jabbed a finger at a scrubby oak tree a few yards away. "Go stand over there."

We followed instructions, lingering under the low branches of the ancient tree while the paramedics loaded Bug into the back of the ambulance. Tobias was looking more shaken than I'd ever seen him.

"Maybe I shouldn't have used the EpiPen," he said. "If he had heart trouble... I may have caused him to have a heart attack."

"He was already struggling when you got to him," I pointed out. "His face was swollen, he couldn't breathe... and besides, his brother said he thought it was an allergic reaction."

"But the EpiPen didn't work," Tobias said.

"Maybe it was a faulty syringe," Peter suggested. "He

asked you to use it; he obviously thought he was having a reaction, too."

I squeezed Tobias's arm. "You didn't do anything wrong," I reiterated. "You can't save everyone."

"I probably shouldn't have done it," he said. "I'm a vet, not a human doctor."

"You were trying to help," I reassured him. "You did what he asked you to do."

"I'm the one who fished it out of the glove compartment," Peter said. "And I'm the one who called PETA to do a demonstration in front of his ranch the other day."

Quinn grabbed Peter's arm. "I'm sure it was just an accident," she said.

I thought of the paper with the dead bee in it and couldn't help but come to a different conclusion, but I didn't say anything. But as I looked over at Mitch Wharton, who was rocking back and forth with his hands in his pockets, his lips in a thin grimace, I wondered how he really felt about his brother's death—and who inherited the game ranch now that Bug was gone.

It was dark by the time we loaded back into the car, any festive feelings long gone. Once we'd answered Rooster's cursory questions, we'd gone back to the ball to try to regain some of the fall magic, but Bug Wharton's death had thrown a pall over things. The crowd had largely dispersed, and no one wanted mead anymore.

"Even in death, he managed to ruin things," Serafine said as we followed her to the house. "This was supposed to be the big fund-raiser for the animal sanctuary, and now everyone's gone home. And Rooster won't let me serve any more mead—not that anyone would drink it."

"They think Bug was poisoned?"

"That's what people are saying," she told me. "I can't believe he had to pick the mead winery to get stung by a bee. I know the mead wasn't poisoned, so that's got to be what happened. I mean, if you're allergic to bees, shouldn't you stay away from them?"

Tobias and I exchanged glances. Serafine didn't seem too upset about Bug's death, that was for sure.

"So instead of promoting my business and helping the animals," Serafine continued, "the whole Witches' Ball backfired on me. Thanks to that stupid Bug Wharton."

She was seething as she unlocked the door and let us into the farmhouse, but her whole demeanor changed as soon as she squatted down next to a large crate by the front door. "How are you doing in there, sweetheart?" she cooed as a little dog with a pink nose came to lick her through the crate's metal grid. She opened the crate and scooped up a small, bald, sore-covered dog. "I think she's looking a little better, don't you?" she asked.

I blinked; if this poor creature was looking better now, I hated to think of what she'd looked like before. Her skin was covered in sores, and her paws were bright red and swollen. "What happened?"

"Neglect," Serafine said as she handed the little dog to Tobias. "Untreated mange and lots of secondary infections."

"Are you giving her the Ivermectin?" Tobias asked as he inspected the little dog.

"I am," she said. "And I'm doing the baths and wiping down her feet, too, just like you suggested. I just wanted you to check on her."

He peered into her eyes, then put her down for a moment and watched as she made a beeline for Serafine, putting her small, swollen paws on the young woman's leg, begging for attention. She bent down and fondled the little dog's ears, then picked her up.

"She looks good to me," he said. "The swelling is going down, and the sores are healing. It will just take time, but if you keep treating her, you should be able to lick the mange. She seems steady on her feet and her eyesight is good, so there are no ill effects from the medication —at least none that I can see. Let me know if she has tremors or seems to have any vision problems."

"I will," she said. "She's such a sweetheart. I know when she's healed, she'll be gorgeous." She rubbed the little dog's head and surveyed the living room, which was covered in boxes of paper cups and napkins; it was obviously a staging area for the Witches' Ball. "We didn't even get to do the costume contest," she said bitterly.

"Maybe we can do a redux closer to Halloween," I suggested.

"We'll see," she replied with a sigh. "I just hope I can make enough to keep things going for the dogs—and for the winery."

"I know the feeling," I told her. "My well dried up."

"Are you sure it's not just a problem with the pump?"

I shook my head. "Lenny doesn't think so; he's coming back tomorrow to talk about options." I sighed. "I think it's time to head home, unless you need a bit of help cleaning up." Peter and Quinn had already taken Flora.

She shook her head. "Aimee and I will deal with it in the morning. I just can't look at it tonight."

"I'm sure everything will look brighter in the morning," Tobias suggested.

"I doubt it, but thanks for the positive thinking," Serafine said grimly.

My cell phone rang just as I finished milking Blossom the next morning. It was Quinn. As I sent the tawny Jersey cow to join her daughter in the pasture and walked toward the house with the milk jug, I hit Talk and held the phone to my ear.

"Any news?" I asked, opening the screen door and stepping into the house that had been my grandmother's when I was a girl.

"He died of an allergic reaction," she said. "Tobias was right about that."

"He'll be relieved," I said, sliding the jug onto the tile counter as my bald poodle, Chuck, nosed at my ankles. Tobias had been uncharacteristically silent on the way home the night before; I knew he felt personally responsible for what had happened to Bug. "But why didn't the EpiPen work?"

"That's the mystery," she said.

"Is Rooster looking in to the bee angle?"

"I don't know," she said. "Mandy Vargas from the Buttercup Zephyr just swung by and asked me a few questions; don't be surprised if you hear from her, too. Oh—and watch out for your livestock. She told me there's word of a chupacabra in the area."

"A what?"

"A chupacabra," she said. "You know, that mythical,

wolflike thing that preys on livestock. A few of the Chovaneks' goats were attacked the other night."

"Oh no!" I said, peering out the window at my little flock, which thankfully seemed to be okay as they nosed the perimeter of their pen. "I'm guessing it's more likely a mountain lion than a chupacabra, though."

"Gus Holz saw something that seemed too weird to be a coyote out by his ranch the other night," Quinn said. "Said his chickens were all upset about something, and he just caught a glimpse of it, but it wasn't like anything he'd seen before."

"Everybody's spooked with Halloween coming up," I said. There had been nothing but ghost stories in town lately... including a juicy one involving the derelict old farmhouse Quinn had convinced me to move onto Dewberry Farm. "Still no ghosts on the Ulrich home-stead, by the way," I informed her. Quinn had talked me into rescuing the hundred-plus-year-old house and moving it to a knoll overlooking Dewberry Creek. I glanced out the farmhouse kitchen window toward the recently relocated house, which was half-obscured by a cottonwood tree.

"I'm so glad you saved it," Quinn said.

"I don't know what I'm going to do with it now that it's here, but at least it won't be demolished," I told her. "It might fall down, but it won't be torn down."

"I told you what to do with it: turn it into a guest-house for when the antique fair is in town. You'll be making money before you know it."

"With all the work that needs doing, it's going to be a while before that house is making any money," I said. Liesl Heinrich's brother, Ralph, had moved the small, wood-frame structure onto the farm for free, but it was up to me to keep the leaning house from falling in on itself. And with a dry well, I wasn't exactly flush with funds for restoration.

"Peter's really good at building; why don't we have him take a look at it?"

"I've got some chicken in the fridge," I mused. "Think you guys would be up for dinner tonight? Maybe we can walk down to the house and he can give me an honest assessment."

"Absolutely!" she said. "We were already planning on dinner together; we'll just head your way. Will Tobias be there, too?"

"I'll ask," I said.

"I've got a pecan pie I just made. Can I bring anything else?"

"Just expertise and reassurance that I'm not crazy for saving the Ulrich house."

"I'm glad you saved it," Quinn repeated. "I just feel like it was meant to be on Dewberry Farm, somehow."

"Let's hope I'm glad, too." At the moment, I was feeling like I'd bitten off way more than I could chew. "Thanks for letting me know about Bug. I'll call Tobias and tell him he was right."

"Are you planning on swinging by the cafe today?" she asked. "I could use a little help at lunch."

"Lenny is supposed to be here at nine to look at the well situation," I said.

"Good luck with that," she said. "Maybe he'll change his mind and tell you it's the pump after all. By the way, any lettuce yet?"

"Still too warm," I said, "but soon, assuming it rains or I get my well squared away." One of the nice things about living in Texas was that there were two growing seasons: the warm season started in March and ran through September, and the cool season picked up when the last of the summer's harvest was drying up. I actually preferred cool-season crops; although I missed having tomatoes and cucumbers, I loved green garlic, fresh lettuce, sugar snap peas, radishes, and particularly arugula. You had to protect some things during harsh cold snaps, but for the most part the winter was as productive—if not more productive—than summer. Right now was a shoulder season; the summer plantings had played out, but the cool-season veggies hadn't matured yet. Plenty of time to tackle the Ulrich house... assuming I got the well fixed and it didn't bankrupt me. If it weren't for my beeswax candles and jams, I wouldn't have much to take to the Saturday market.

"Well, I'll let you get your chores done," Quinn said. "We'll definitely be there tonight. Come by the cafe today if you can!"

"I'll try," I said and hung up a moment later. Between the well fiasco and the leaning haunted house, I certainly did need all the extra work I could get. I called Tobias and left a message, then turned to my morning chores.

I'd just finished processing the milk when the phone rang again; it was Tobias.

"You were right," I told him as I put the last jar of milk into the fridge. "Quinn called; Bug Wharton died of anaphylaxis."

"At least I didn't misdiagnose it," he said. "But the EpiPen should have worked."

"Maybe we got there too late?"

"Maybe," he said, but didn't sound convinced. "What are you up to today?"

"Lenny Froehlich is coming out to talk about the well this morning," I said, "and then Quinn wants me to swing by the Blue Onion if I have time. And I was hoping you would join Peter, Quinn, and me for pot pie tonight."

"I'd love to," he said. "But what are you doing before that?"

"Why?"

"I'm supposed to head out to the Safari Exotic Game Ranch to check on some ibexes at two," he told me. "I was wondering if you wanted to tag along."

"Ibexes?"

"They just came in from Africa," he said. "Plus, I thought you might be curious to take a look at the place."

"I kind of am," I confessed. My reporter instincts were telling me what had happened to Bug was no accident; I was anxious to take a look at the Wharton place from the inside.

"I hope the well problem gets fixed soon; let me know what he says. Can I pick you up at the Blue Onion at one-thirty?"

"Sounds like a plan," I said, and hung up with a new spring in my step. "Maybe it's not such a bad day after all, Chuck," I said to my bald poodle, who wagged in response and licked my calf.

Ha.

Chapter 3

"YOUR OPTIONS," LENNY FROEHLICH TOLD me as we stood over my bone-dry well, "are to drill deeper and hope we get lucky, or drill a whole new well."

"Okay," I said. "What's the benefit of a new well?"

"More water, hopefully," he said.

"How much is that going to cost?"

"I won't lie to you; both are gonna cost you a pretty penny," he told me. "But if you do drill a new well, the question is, where do we put it?"

"Ideally, where there's water," I said. "But how do you know?"

"Well, that's where the dowser comes in," he said.

"The dowser?"

He nodded. "Water witch, they used to call 'em. He could always sniff out the best spot to drill. Problem is, the dowser—Gusher Orton—died last year."

"Gusher?"

"Name was Gus, but he was always good at findin' water, so the nickname kind of stuck."

Unfortunately for me, Gus wasn't around anymore, so I couldn't take advantage of his magical skills. "So, what do we do without a dowser?"

He shrugged. "Just start drillin' and hope for the best."

"Surely there's some other way to do it?"

"I'll look in to it and get back to you," he told me, not meeting my eyes.

"What do I do in the meantime?"

"A few things. You can spend the money to get a tank of water out here," he said.

"That doesn't sound cheap. Any other options?"

He glanced up at the cloudless sky. "Pray for rain."

"Do you know anyone who can dowse a well?" I asked Quinn as I walked into the kitchen of the Blue Onion later that morning.

"Only one I know of was Gusher Orton," she told me as she tossed a big bowl of salad, "and he passed."

"That's what Lenny said." I sighed and tied on an apron, taking an appreciative sniff of the fresh-bread-scented air. It was a good thing I got a lot of exercise out at the farm, or I'd be the size of a house with all the day-old baked goods I took home from the cafe. "I guess I'm going to have to truck in some water while I get it figured out, although I have no idea how to go about doing that. I've got to have something for the animals to drink—and to water my seedlings."

"I'll see what I can find out for you," Quinn said.

"I guess I can't do anything about it right now," I said glumly.

"We'll work it out. Maybe Peter can help; the fire department's got a pumper truck."

"That might work as a stopgap," I agreed, feeling a slight ray of hope. "Need me in front today?"

"That'd be great," Quinn told me as I grabbed a pad and pushed through the swinging door to the front of the cafe.

The Blue Onion was a fixture on Buttercup's Town Square. With Quinn's charming touches—a mix of antique tables and chairs, white curtains, and refinished pecan floors, along with little vases of flowers on each table—it was a haven of hominess and comfort. The delicious breads and sweets in the glass case by the register and the yeasty aroma of baked goods wafting through the air had won Quinn a loyal customer base, and although it was early for lunch, the little cafe was bustling.

I spent the next hour and a half taking orders and half-listening to the gossip about Bug Wharton's recent demise out at the Honeyed Moon winery.

"I heard it was that potion she served up that did him in," Max Gunther, a retired rancher, said as he swilled iced tea.

"Oh, nonsense," his wife Jean said. "It was honey wine, not bee venom. Besides, I heard he was stung on the way back to his truck."

"I'll bet they put a spell on him because they didn't like him shootin' all those exotic deer. You were there when it happened, weren't you?" Max asked, narrowing his eyes at me. "You see any funny business?"

"It was very sad," I told him, "but evidently it was just an allergic reaction. Anaphylactic shock can happen very fast."

"I just don't know," he said. "I still think those witchy women are involved."

His wife just rolled her eyes and ignored him as I refilled their drinks and moved on to the next table, which was inhabited by Maria Ulrich, one of the members of the town's German Club. She didn't look very German—she had her Mexican mother's silky black hair and dark eyes—but she was proud of her heritage on both sides. Maria was lunching with another German Club member, Liesl Heinrich.

"Lucy!" Maria said. "I hear you moved the old Ulrich homestead out to your farm. Thank you so much for saving it. Our family came over in the early eighteen hundreds and were very active in the town."

"Quinn mentioned that to me," I told her.

"I can't wait to see what it looks like when you've restored it," Maria said. "It's hard to imagine my family lived there; it seems like another world."

"I hope I'll be able to save it," I told her. "I just found out my well's run dry. I'm not sure I'm going to be able to afford much to restore it."

"Oh, I'm so sorry to hear that," Liesl said, turning to Maria. "Maybe the club can help out a bit? After all, it is a historic building."

"When was it built anyway?" I asked.

"A couple of years after they got here," Maria told me. "They raised six children in that house. Can you believe it?"

"No, I really can't," I said, thinking of the small, ramshackle house down by the creek. It was barely big enough for a couple by today's standards, never mind a family of eight.

"It was my great-great-great-great-grandfather—I think that's enough greats, anyway—who built it," Maria told me. "And my great-great-great-great-grandmother did the blue stenciling all around the tops of the walls."

"That's my favorite part of the house!" I said. The downstairs walls were made of boards that had been painted white with a china-blue pattern stenciled around the perimeter.

"I'm so glad it's not being destroyed," Liesl said. "It has such potential, and, of course, lots of history."

"I heard about that," I replied. "And I've heard it's supposed to be haunted, too."

Maria and Liesl exchanged looks; evidently, they'd heard that story, too. "Well, it does have some history," Maria admitted.

"What kind of history?" I asked, a little irritated no one had mentioned the haunting to me before I agreed to have the house deposited on my property.

"One of their children—a teenage daughter named Ilse—disappeared."

"What happened to her?"

She shrugged. "Nobody knows; she was never heard from again."

"So, is the ghost supposed to be your grandparent, or the missing girl?"

They glanced at each other again. "Nobody knows for sure, but rumor has it it's the ghost of Ilse. My grandmother said she saw her once, in the upstairs window," Maria admitted.

"Still, it's an adorable house," Liesl put in quickly.

"It is," Maria agreed. "I'd have taken the house myself, but I live in town, and I don't really have any land to put it on."

"It's a cute little house," I told her. And it was; it was a simple, small, cozy farmhouse, with a front porch that invited rocking chairs—assuming the porch didn't cave in when you stepped on it. "I hope the ghost—if there is one—doesn't object to visitors. The only way I can afford to preserve it is if I can rent it out."

"I'm sorry we didn't tell you," Maria said. "It's just... it seemed like the perfect location for it."

"We'll see what we can do to help," Liesl rushed to

add. "We'll take it up with the club."

I sighed. What was done was done. And it was a cute house, despite its history. "If you know anyone who can help with my well, I'd appreciate that, too."

"With the drought, lots of folks are having water problems," Maria said. "Happening more and more the last few years."

"Maybe this wasn't the best time to take up farming."

"There's never a perfect time to do anything," Maria said. "Sometimes you just have to take the plunge."

Like buying a haunted house that was falling in on itself, I thought grimly as I refilled their iced tea and headed back to the kitchen.

I had just cashed out my last check when Tobias walked into the Blue Onion, wearing jeans and a faded blue T-shirt that stretched over his chest and biceps in a way that made my heart skip a few beats.

"Hey," he said with a slow smile that did nothing to help my heart rate. I reached up to adjust my hair and found myself wishing I'd put on a bit of makeup before leaving the farm that morning.

"You about ready?" he asked.

"I am. Let me just get my purse." I ducked into the back, shed my apron, and told Quinn Tobias had arrived and that we were heading over to Bug Wharton's place.

"It seems so weird that they pay for a vet to make sure the animals are okay when all they're going to do is shoot them," she said.

"It does seem strange," I acknowledged. "But I'm really curious about what that place looks like on the inside."

"You're still thinking about what happened to Bug Wharton, aren't you?"

"Yeah. I just have a feeling there's something funny going on."

"I hope not," Quinn said as she slipped a batch of maple twists into the oven. "We were first at the scene—and Tobias was the one who used the EpiPen. I'd hate to see Rooster go after him for being a Good Samaritan."

"Why would Tobias want to hurt Bug Wharton?" I asked. In truth, Peter was the one who had organized the PETA protest—and it was Peter who had gotten the EpiPen out of the glove compartment. A little squiggle of worry stirred in my stomach.

"I don't think logic has anything to do with Rooster's thinking process," Quinn pointed out.

"Unfortunately, you're right," I told her as I hung up the apron and grabbed my purse.

"Have fun," she said. "I can't wait to hear what you think about it!"

"I'll let you know," I promised her as I pushed through the swinging door into the cafe, where Tobias was ogling the bakery case.

"How do you spend time here and not gain fifty pounds?" he asked.

"Because I'm always on the move," I said, grinning.

Tobias gave me a quick kiss on the top of the head, then tore himself away from the case and held the door to the cafe open for me. "Ready to visit Little Africa?"

"Who knew we'd be on safari in Buttercup?"

"It's an adventure every day," he said, winking as I climbed into the truck.

It was a short, pleasant ride to the Safari Exotic Game

Ranch. I filled Tobias in on my nonexistent well progress as we drove past bleached fields and farmhouses with pumpkins and chrysanthemums adorning their front porches. Tobias seemed quiet, I noticed.

"What's wrong?" I asked.

"I'm still thinking about what happened to Bug Wharton," he told me. "I could have misdiagnosed him. It happened so fast..."

"He asked for the EpiPen and you gave it to him," I said. "You weren't diagnosing anything; you were doing what he asked you to do. Besides, it was anaphylaxis."

"But he died," Tobias said. "I just can't get it out of my mind."

"Maybe there was something wrong with the EpiPen," I said. "I read an article recently about a recall. At any rate, it really doesn't matter. You had nothing to do with what happened to Bug Wharton. If anything, I'm wondering if someone had it in for him."

"What do you mean?"

"It looked to me like someone slipped some bees in a twist of paper through a crack in the window," I said. "I wonder who owns the ranch?"

"Are you thinking someone might have done him in to inherit?" Tobias asked.

"It's total speculation," I said. "We don't even have a cause of death yet. It was probably just an accident."

"I hope you're right." He grimaced as he turned onto the road that led to the ranch. "But there's something off about the whole thing."

"Unfortunately, I think I have to agree with you," I said as we bumped down the dirt road.

Unlike most of the ranches in Buttercup, the Safari Exotic Game Ranch was ringed with a shiny, ten-foot-high fence. "How many acres is the ranch, anyway?" I asked as I watched for signs of exotic animals in the scrubby oaks and mesquite trees.

"It's pretty big," he said. "At least a couple thousand acres."

"That must have cost a fortune." I had had to stretch to buy my own small piece of property; the Wharton clan must have deep pockets. "Are game ranches profitable?"

"They can be," he said. "People spend tens of thousands of dollars for a trophy hunt."

"Tens of thousands of dollars just to shoot an animal? I don't get it."

"Me neither," he said. "I know Peter's against the whole thing on principle, but there are folks who argue these game ranches are kind of a living ark of sorts, and that the hunters provide the money to keep the genetic diversity alive."

"It still seems messed up," I said as we pulled up to the enormous metal gates. "And I still wonder what business they were in to afford all this."

"Bug told me they grew up in Buttercup, but I don't know what they did before moving back."

"Whatever it was, it looks like it was pretty lucrative," I said as Tobias rolled down the window and hit the intercom button. A moment later, the gates opened, and we rolled into the property.

As we followed the long, winding gravel road, I spotted a herd of something with long, backward-pointing horns to the left. They barely moved as we drove by; the biggest switched his tail, but otherwise they seemed unconcerned. "What are they?" I asked.

"Gazelles," Tobias said.

"Not exactly shy, are they?"

"No predators here." He sighed. "Before he died, Bug told me he'd got some kangaroos coming in, too."

"Kangaroos?"

Tobias nodded, his face grim. "And a pair of giraffes. That's what the animal-rights activists were complaining about."

"That's horrible!" I said. "Who would want to shoot a kangaroo or a giraffe?"

"I know," he said. "I almost refused to treat the animals, but I don't want them to get sick or suffer any more than they have to. It's a dilemma."

My eyes drifted to the gazelles. "They're totally unconcerned about us."

"Because they're raised by people. They're essentially tame animals."

"Who are in for a big surprise, unfortunately." My heart hurt at the thought of shooting these beautiful animals.

"It's sad, but it's legal."

"I don't feel quite so bad about Bug now," I admitted. We fell silent for a minute; then I changed the subject, telling him about what Maria had related about the house.

"It's really haunted?"

"That's what they say," I told him.

"Superstition's running high this year, it seems. There's also word of a chupacabra running around," Tobias told me.

"I heard about that," I said. "What do you think it is?"

"Probably a coyote," Tobias said. "Keep an eye on everybody at your place; you might want to put them in at night for a while, just in case." As he spoke, we turned a bend, and the main compound of the ranch came into view.

"Nice place," I said, admiring the large log cabins arrayed around a small lake, along with a low-slung main building with a long front porch and an expensive-looking metal roof.

"It is," he said, following a small dirt road past the compound. Beyond a stand of trees was a barn and a few large pens in which a few animals with huge, curved horns huddled under a shelter. "What are those?" I asked.

"They're the animals I'm supposed to look at, I imagine," he said. "They just brought them in from Africa."

He pulled up under a tree and cut the engine, and as we got out of the truck, a wiry man in jeans, scuffed boots, and a straw hat walked over to the car.

"Hey, José," Tobias greeted him, shaking his callused hand. "How's it going?"

"Not too bad, considering," José answered.

"I'm sorry about your boss," he said.

José shrugged. "It's life. I just hope I still have a job."

"Has the sheriff been by at all?" he asked.

"Not that I know of," José said. "But the other Mr. Wharton would be the person to ask about that."

He was very guarded about his bosses, evidently. As I walked around the truck, Tobias put an arm around my shoulder. "This is my girlfriend, Lucy Resnick. Lucy, José."

"Nice to meet you," I said, shaking his callused hand. His face was tanned and weathered, and his dark eyes were quick and intelligent.

"José's in charge of all the animals here; he's been caring for livestock since he was a boy. Lucy's just starting a farm of her own."

"Hard work," he said, and I couldn't disagree. "What

animals?" he asked.

"Two cows, four goats, and some chickens," I told him.

"Goats are very clever," he said. "You have to watch them."

"So's one of my cows," I said. "She likes to head to town every chance she gets."

"We've had a few escapees here, too," José said, his words slightly accented. "Someone's been cutting the fences."

"When did that start happening?" Tobias asked.

"A few weeks ago," he said. "Mr. Wharton thought it must be those protestors, or the witch ladies. They don't like the ranch very much."

"I gathered," Tobias said. "Did you get all the animals back?"

"They didn't go far," he said. "And they always come back for corn. The new ones are over here," he told Tobias, waving him toward a small pen in the lee of the barn. Three tawny animals with long horns were huddled against the side of the barn, looking nervous.

As Tobias unlocked the gate, I hung back. "I don't want to freak them out any more," I said.

"I'd feel safer with you out here anyway," he said.

I hung over the side of the fence as he and José approached the animals, talking softly so as not to scare them. They shuffled and snorted a little bit, but the two men exuded such calm and confidence they didn't run. As José put one hand on the smallest ibex's nose and talked to her in lilting Spanish, Tobias quickly did an exam. José fed her a carrot as Tobias took blood, and then they moved on to the next animal. Within twenty minutes, they had finished, and the animals frisked around a little as José and Tobias let themselves back out.

"They look good," Tobias said. "Are they eating well?"

"Not for the first few days, but they're settling in now."

"Do you have their papers?"

"In the office," José said. "Hold on; I'll get them."

As he loped off in the direction of a small trailer tucked behind the barn, I leaned over the fence and watched the animals. "I can't imagine wanting to shoot one of them."

"I know," he said. "It's strange checking their health when I know they're going to be... well, harvested. I guess it's the same with livestock, though."

As he spoke, there was the sound of raised voices from not far away. I put a hand on Tobias's arm and pulled him closer to the barn.

Chapter 4

"I TOLD YOU WE WERE DONE," a woman said. The voice was familiar. "Please give them back to me."

A man's wheedling voice answered. "You wouldn't have come here if you didn't want to be together."

"I don't want to be together," she said. "I just came to pick up my things."

"But sweetheart," he said, "we were so good together."

"It was a mistake. Just give me my stuff back..."

"Just one last kiss?"

Tobias and I exchanged glances. I peered around the side of the barn, but I couldn't see anyone.

"No. Leave me alone!"

"You came here," he said. "Besides, why would you want to go now? I told you, I'm right on the edge of making it big."

"I don't want anything from you," she said. "I'm leaving now. Good-bye."

"But honey..."

I risked another peek around the barn, but I couldn't see anyone, and there were no more voices. A moment later, José came back, carrying a sheaf of papers. "Finally found them," he told us. "I made copies for you." He looked up from the papers and noticed we were both crouched against the barn. "What's going on?"

"Oh, there was a bit of a lovers' tiff," I said. "We didn't want to interrupt."

José's weathered face went blank, and he glanced over his shoulder. "Oh. I don't know anything about that." As he spoke, there was the sound of a car engine revving, and the screech of tires. I caught a glimpse of a small green car stirring up a cloud of dust; then it was gone.

"Somebody's leaving in a hurry. Whose car is that?" I asked.

José shrugged. "I didn't see," he said, and handed Tobias the papers. "When will we know about the blood test?"

"I'll call you as soon as I hear," he said. "Again, so sorry to hear about your boss."

"Thank you," he said. "Nice to meet you, Miss Resnick," he said, nodding at me.

"Likewise," I told him.

"Mind if I show her some of the other animals?" Tobias asked.

José looked nervous. "It might be best if you didn't," he told Tobias. "With everything going on, and the new animals..." He shrugged. "Maybe another time."

"It's okay," Tobias said. "Thanks."

As he spoke, Bug Wharton's brother Mitch rounded the barn. "José, you haven't mucked out the stalls yet," he complained in a familiar voice. It was the same man we'd heard a few minutes before, cajoling an unknown woman.

Tobias and I exchanged glances as José answered, "I'm about to take care of it, Mr. Wharton. I was just helping Dr. Brandt with the ibexes."

"Dr. Brandt; always good to see you."

"Likewise; I'm sorry about your brother."

"Bad luck," he said, shaking his head. "It still hasn't really sunk in yet." Mitch seemed bigger, somehow, than he had when he was standing next to Bug the other day. "How's the livestock looking?"

"In good shape, from what I can see," Tobias said. "Have you met my girlfriend, Lucy Resnick?" he asked.

"Pleased to meet you," he said, extending his ham-like hand to me. I shook it, wincing as he crushed my knuckles.

"I'm so sorry about your brother," I said.

"Thank you, ma'am. We're still tryin' to come to terms with it. This whole ranch was the dream of a lifetime for him. Shame he didn't get to enjoy it."

"It is. It's a beautiful place," Tobias said politely,

Mitch turned to the animals huddled in their pen. "Got a whole crew comin' all the way from Dallas this weekend," he said. "These won't be ready yet," he said, nodding at the ibexes huddled in the pen, "but we've got more oryxes than you can shake a stick at. Big racks, too."

"I've never seen an oryx before," I said.

"I'll take you out to see them," he said in a jovial tone. If he was sad about his brother, he was certainly hiding it well. "Come on; I'll give you a ride on the ATV."

I glanced over at José, who didn't look happy, but didn't argue.

"Okay," I said, and Tobias and I followed him across the courtyard to a carport with three shiny ATVs.

"Hop in," he said, and Tobias and I slid into the backseat of the nearest one while he clambered into the front and gunned the engine. I had to hold on to Tobias as he jerked the vehicle into reverse, then swung past a dismayed-looking José and into one of the pastures.

"It's a gorgeous property," Tobias said as we drove past a bend in a dry creek. Even though the ground was parched, the rolling hills, grassland, and scattered trees made for a beautiful landscape. I shivered as a gust from the north swept over the pasture, making the bleached grass ripple like the surface of a golden lake.

"It is, isn't it? My brother just fell in love with the views," he said. "It was his baby, not mine. Sad the way it worked out." For the first time, I heard something like regret in his voice.

"Do you think you'll keep the place?" Tobias asked.

"We'll see," he answered. "Look there," he said excitedly. "There's a herd of oryxes." The graceful creatures looked up, unperturbed, and then went back to grazing. "They'll make good hunting this weekend," he said.

"How much per head?" Tobias asked.

"Ten thousand," he said proudly. "If we keep getting business the way it's been going, the place might just turn a profit."

I watched as one of the oryxes nosed at her calf, pushing her away from the ATV. It made me sad to think of the little herd being stalked by a family bristling with guns.

"This was a cattle ranch before, wasn't it?" Tobias asked.

"Two of them, in fact," Mitch answered. "We got lucky."

"A lot of property to fence," Tobias said. "How many animals do you have out here, anyway?"

"I lose track," he said as he zoomed close enough to the animals to startle them. I watched as the mother shepherded her little one away from the ATV again, feeling angry at Mitch for spooking the herd for the fun of it.

For the next twenty minutes, he drove us through the ranch, taking hard turns and seemingly enjoying scaring the animals. "It makes the hunts a little more challenging," he explained. As he jerkily rounded a bend, I spotted something in the tall grass.

"Tobias," I said, grabbing his arm and pointing.

"Stop the ATV," he said. "There's a hurt animal."

"Where?" Mitch asked, jerking the vehicle to a sudden stop. Tobias jumped out and hurried over to the tawny oryx half-hidden by tufts of grass.

"She's still alive, at least," he said, kneeling by her head. "But something got to her."

I gasped at the claw marks and puncture wounds on her left flank; they looked incredibly painful. Blood pooled on the parched ground beneath her.

Tobias did a quick examination, then looked up at Mitch. "Has anything like this happened before?"

Mitch shook his head. "Not that I've seen."

"I'm going to need to take her back to the clinic," Tobias said. "This is more than I can handle in the field."

"She's worth a pretty penny," Mitch said, "so do what you can."

"Lucy, can you stay with her while I get my bag? I'd like to get some painkillers into her, and maybe a sedative. Moving her is going to hurt; I don't want her to flail and do more damage."

"Will do," I said, sitting down next to the wounded animal and trying to exude calming energy. Her eyes were wide, and her body was twitching; it was obvious she was in terrible pain. "How long ago did this happen, do you think?"

"I'm guessing it's been a few hours," Tobias said. "I'm going to get the truck. I don't think she'll try to go anywhere. Can you stay with her for just a few minutes?"

"What if... whatever it is comes back?" I asked.

"Take this," Mitch said, pulling a shotgun from the back of the ATV.

"I don't know how to use it," I told him.

"I think I'd feel better if you stayed with Lucy," Tobias said. "I'll come back with the truck."

Tobias's take-charge tone brooked no argument. Mitch handed him the keys, and a moment later, he was speeding back toward the truck. It was only when he was out of sight that it occurred to me that I might have preferred being left on my own. I felt a stir of discomfort in my stomach; I knew there was something fishy about Bug Wharton's death, and realized I might be more comfortable facing a mountain lion alone than Mitch Wharton.

I stroked the oryx's head, feeling nervous, and tried to make conversation. "How long have you been in the ranching business?" I asked.

"We just bought the place last year," he said. "Bug always wanted a ranch."

"I'm so sorry about what happened," I said.

"He always said, when your ticket's up, it's up."

"What did you do before you got into ranching?"

"Oh, Bug was into computers," he said vaguely. Which surprised me; he hadn't seemed like the bearded, mismatched-sock, high-tech type.

"Was he with a start-up?" I asked, thinking that would explain how he was able to afford a sprawling ranch.

"Nah," Mitch said. "Worked for a couple of agencies."

"Kind of a big transition, moving to the country."

"We grew up in the country," he told me.

"Oh, really?"

"Just up the road," he told me. "In Smithville."

"You must have missed it," I said. The poor oryx flailed a little. I put a hand on its shoulder and cooed at it as Mitch answered my question.

"We did. It's just too bad Bug isn't around to enjoy it. It was his idea to come back, after all."

"Was it?"

"Finally able to afford a ranch, and now... this." He shifted the gun from hand to hand.

"You're thinking of keeping it, though."

"I don't know," he said, and I got the distinct feeling he didn't want to talk about it. "We'll have to see how it shakes out."

"It's got to be really tough," I said.

"At least there's plenty to keep me busy," he said. "There's this attack... and then somebody's been poaching lately."

"Poaching?"

"It's all I can think of. We've lost a few head lately."

"Could be a mountain lion," I suggested."

"A mountain lion can't drag a whole oryx off the property," he said.

"Are they shooting them, or stealing them?"

He shrugged. "It's a big property." Before he could say more, he was interrupted by the sound of Tobias's truck. The oryx's nostrils flared, and the whites showed around her eyes.

"It's okay," I crooned as Tobias hurried over to her. He injected her with an anesthetic. When she relaxed, together we loaded her into the back of the truck. "I'll give you a ride back to the entrance. Want to go with me to the clinic?"

"Afraid I'm booked this afternoon," Mitch said. "Got some clients coming in. Can you get her there without me? I've got a trailer you can borrow."

"That'll work," Tobias said.

"Send me the bill," Mitch said blithely.

I hoped Tobias would double it.

Chapter 5

"MITCH WHARTON'S A JERK," I announced to Tobias once we'd gotten the oryx stitched up and settled. I'd helped him out with the surgery, scrubbing up and handing him tools as he needed them because his assistant was out on a call. It wasn't my favorite thing to do, but I'd learned a few things.

"He is a jerk," Tobias agreed as he did a last check on the bandages, "but I try to take care of the animals."

"Do you think he did in his brother?"

He stood up and stepped away from the oryx, who was still sedated. "No way to know. But he didn't seem too broken up about it."

"I wonder what Bug's will looks like."

"You thinking about that conversation with the mystery woman?" Tobias asked as he let himself out of the oryx's stall.

"I am. He told her he could give her anything she wanted now. I wonder who she was?"

"Whoever it was, she certainly wasn't buying it, was she?"

"No, but he has something she wanted."

"All kinds of mystery," Tobias said. "And I'm sure you'll find out."

"I hope so," I said. "I have a bad feeling about this."

"Have you talked to the folks over at the winery

since it happened?"

"No," I said, "but I'm thinking about it."

"It'd be worth looking in to," he said.

"I think so, too. I just wish I knew what was in that will."

"I'll bet Quinn could find out."

He was probably right. "You don't think this was an accident either, do you?" I asked him.

He shook his head. "I'm worried about Peter, to be honest. Rooster can't stand him—thinks he's an Austin hippie—and he and Bug had a shouting match at the protest just last week."

"And then Aimee pulled that death card..." It wasn't looking good.

"I'm not saying Rooster's going to arrest Peter—I'm not sure how you call anaphylactic shock murder—but I think it might be smart to ask around a little bit, just so there's some other plausible explanation in case he does."

"If someone planted bees and tampered with the EpiPen, I'd say that sounds like murder."

"I hadn't thought of that," Tobias said. "It would explain why it wouldn't work."

"Was the truck locked?" I asked.

"I have no idea," he said.

"It doesn't matter that much, really; if someone knew he kept it in the glove compartment, they could have tampered with it at any time."

Tobias nodded. "And then picked a good moment to make sure he got stung."

"He was at the ball; the whole town was there. Everyone knew he and Peter had argued."

"He and Serafine tangled, too," Tobias reminded me. "So, lots of options if you wanted to throw people off your scent."

"I think I may need to go talk with Serafine and Aimee."

"I'd go with you, but I need to keep an eye on her while she's recovering. Call when you get back, okay?."

"I will. I still haven't dealt with the well, either," I realized suddenly.

"Stop by Peter's on the way," he suggested. "Maybe he can fill up the pumper truck for you."

"It's worth a shot," I said. "I'll do that."

He gave me a kiss as I headed toward the door. "Keep me posted."

Peter wasn't home, unfortunately, so I headed on to visit Serafine and Aimee.

The Honeyed Moon winery looked just as magical in the daytime as it had at the ball. The cauldron was gone from the fire pit, but the pumpkins and straw bales remained in the courtyard between the barn and the farmhouse. Chrysanthemums spilled out of pots by the front door of the barn—the winery's main working space—and a tangle of queen's wreath climbed up the side of the building, a profusion of blooms swaying in the light breeze. Clumps of Mexican bush sage bloomed rich purple, and the soft, velvety flowers were buzzing with bees. A sweet, honeyed smell hung in the air, and I could hear the sound of humming from the barn.

"Hello?" I called as I approached the big double doors, which were ajar.

"Come in!" I recognized Serafine's voice.

"It's Lucy," I said as I stepped into the cool, sweet-scented interior of the barn.

"You've got perfect timing," Serafine said as she fitted a small valve-looking object to the top of a big glass jug. The air smelled intoxicating; in addition to honey, there was a lingering scent of summer peaches. She was working at a big, wooden farm table in the middle of the barn. The space was outfitted with several tables, a variety of enormous pots, something that looked like a stove, an assortment of intimidating-looking—to me, anyway—equipment, and a few funnels. There were racks of empty bottles and several rolls of Serafine's hand-designed Honeyed Moon labels. "I'm just finishing up this batch of melomel."

"What's melomel?"

"It's a mead flavored with fruit," Serafine said as she stepped back to observe her work: a dozen glass jugs filled with amber liquid. Despite last night's fiasco, I was glad to see that she seemed to be in good spirits. She wiped her hands on her overalls, and I found myself envying her. Even with the old work boots and faded overalls, her gorgeous pile of braided hair and her flawless skin made her look exotic and beautiful. "We put up a lot of the peach harvest as puree in the spring so that we can make it all year round. It's one of my favorites," she said. "Customers like it, too; one of the stores in Austin sells out almost as fast as we can make it."

"How long does it take to make?"

"Now that it's mixed, it'll take three rackings—three or four months—before it's done," she said. "We keep everything in a climate-controlled room in the back of the barn and label it so we don't lose track of it. Here... come help me put these carboys in and I'll show you."

"Carboys?"

"That's what these glass containers are," she informed me as she lugged one onto a cart. "It's what we use to ferment the mead."

I grasped one of the warm jugs and slid it onto the cart. "A lot of people use plastic, but we like to use glass. We're on the lookout for more used equipment; we're trying to expand."

"That's great news," I said. "Are you sure you can spare me the bees in the spring?"

"Of course," she said as she loaded another carboy onto the cart. "We've found a supplier for the honey; she's giving it to us at a really good price, and it's delicious stuff. All local."

"Think she'd be interested in supplying beeswax, too?" I asked. Beeswax candles were one of my most popular market items.

"I'll ask," she said.

Together, we finished loading the carboys onto the cart, and I watched as Serafine tied a label to each of them. "What are those for?" I asked.

"They tell me what it is and when it was made," she said. "When you make as much mead as we do, you have to keep track. I put it on my calendar, too, so I have a master list." She slid the last jug onto the cart, then walked over and opened the sealed door to the back half of the barn. "Ready?" she asked, switching on a light, and I followed her and the cart into the dark, wine-scented storage room.

The walls were lined with jugs. Some were cloudy, some were clear, and the colors ranged from golden to deep berry red. "Wow," I said. "That's a lot of mead. What do you do when you bottle it?"

"We keep it back here," she said, pointing to a stack of crates I hadn't noticed. "Most we bottle; we keep a few in carboys for events like the ball. Aimee is sanitizing the ones we used so we can use them again." She pulled a face. "And of course they took some of our stuff after what happened to Bug Wharton."

"What?" I asked.

"For evidence," she said, quirking her mouth to the side. "Although it doesn't make any sense to me. I heard he died of a bee sting. Just because you're allergic to bee stings doesn't mean you'll have a reaction to honey. Besides," she added, "if he was worried about it, he shouldn't have had any."

"You weren't too crazy about him, were you?"

"No," she said shortly as she washed her hands at a big sink. "Our views on animals were about as opposite as you can get. He raises them as objects to be hunted. I try to save them from being mistreated."

"I was just out there this morning. One of their animals was attacked by what looked like a coyote or a mountain lion," I told her. "I don't know if they go after dogs, but you might want to keep an eye out."

"I did hear a ruckus the other night," she said, "but whatever spooked everyone was gone by the time I got outside. Speaking of dogs," she said, "I've got to feed everyone and medicate one of them. Aimee was supposed to be back by now, but there's no sign of her. Would you mind giving me a hand?"

"I'd be happy to," I said, following her out of the barn, a little surprised when she locked the door behind her.

"I know it's weird in Buttercup," she said, "but mead's alcoholic. Someone broke in not too long ago. Didn't do much damage, but a couple of things disappeared."

"Nothing valuable, I hope?"

"I don't think so, but they did lift a few cases of mead. Probably teenagers. So now I lock things up when I leave."

She pocketed the key and headed to a small building next to the farmhouse. As she approached, there
was a raucous chorus of barking, accompanied by a
number of wagging tails. A three-legged yellow Lab,
a scruffy-looking black Scottie, and a gray German
shepherd trotted up to greet Serafine as she opened
the gate and walked into the yard. The Scottie stood
up on her hind legs, begging to be picked up; Serafine ruffled her head with a laugh. "She's small, but she
holds her own with everyone," she said. "If I could, I'd
have them all in the house, but there'd be no room for
me on the bed!"

"I understand," I said, thinking of Chuck, who took
up an awful lot of space for a poodle. I often found
myself relegated to six inches of bed—sometimes less.

We walked into the small house, which was outfitted with an overstuffed couch, a chair, and a very
basic kitchenette. A giant bin of dog food stood on the
counter, along with a basket of various medications,
and there were at least fifteen crates in the room, most
unoccupied. I helped her feed everyone, then waited as
she called the outside dogs in and sent out three more.

"Where's the sick one?" I asked.

"In the house," she said. "She's not ready for all this
yet; she's still recovering."

I followed her out of the sanctuary and across the
yard to the farmhouse she shared with her sister. Like
Serafine, the house was decorated in a fun, quirky
manner, with a hanging string of crystals and mirrors
and a gaily colored metal rooster on the front porch. I
followed her into the house, which smelled of spices
and roses—not, thankfully, dog—and into the kitchen,
where the small white dog I'd seen the day before was

curled on a fluffy dog bed.

At least I think it was a dog; it was shaved, and looked more like a scabby goat.

"Hey, Chiquis," she said in a soft voice. The little dog looked up at her with big brown eyes, trembling.

"How did she end up with that horrible skin infection?" I asked.

"Neglect," Serafine said. "The shelter called me last week to come and get her; she's got mange, secondary skin infections, worms, the works."

"That's horrible," I said.

"I know," she told me, picking up the little dog. "She's been this way for more than a year, too; the family tried to surrender her last September. I think they were just struggling to get by. The shelter gave them funds to use at a vet, but they only used sixty dollars of it, so she's suffered for at least twelve months."

"Is it fixable?" I asked.

"Yes," she said. "It's just time-consuming. She's worth it, though, aren't you?" she cooed as she lifted the little dog. "Can you hold her while I give her her medicine?"

"Sure," I said as she handed me the little dog, who weighed maybe ten pounds. She had a mousy smell to her.

"What's the smell?" I asked.

"Unfortunately, it's the mange," she said, wrinkling her nose. "I'll give her another special bath tonight; it helps her skin heal and makes her feel more comfortable." As I watched, she measured out some fluid into a syringe and walked over to me.

"There's a good girl," she cooed as she slipped it into Chiquis's mouth. "I know it tastes bad, but it will make you feel better." She put down the syringe and gave the little dog a bit of cheese, which she gulped down.

Chiquis had just finished her treat when the door opened, and Serafine's sister, Aimee, walked in. "I talked to..." she started, then spotted me and stopped short. "Oh. Hi."

"Hey, sis. Lucy was just helping me medicate Chiquis," Serafine told her. "And I just finished making the peach melomel," she added with an edge to her voice.

"Sorry I was late getting back," Aimee said, her eyes sliding over to me. She wore a long blue gypsy-style skirt, a gray crop top, and a sparkly blue jacket; she looked more like she was dressed for a date in Austin than work at a winery in Buttercup.

"No problem," Serafine said. "There's plenty more to do... I haven't cleaned out the chicken coop yet."

Aimee let out a big sigh, sounding just like a teenager. She opened her mouth as if she were going to say something, then glanced at me and thought better of it. The kitchen seemed to fill up with unspoken words.

"I'm going to show Lucy the hives," Serafine said, getting up abruptly. Chiquis trembled in my lap; she seemed to be fairly sensitive to what was going on around her. I stroked her scabby head, and she settled down. Poor thing; she really did look like a goat. She didn't smell so hot, either, but I knew it wasn't her fault.

"I'll take her," Serafine said. I relinquished the little dog to her, and she gently replaced her on her bed. Chiquis looked up at me with scared brown eyes, then curled up in a tiny ball.

"Poor baby," I said.

"I know. It's terrible what people put animals through," Serafine said gently. "At any rate, let's go look at the hives!"

Serafine paused to remind her sister about the chicken coop, but Aimee said nothing; she just pressed her lips together.

"Man," Serafine said when the door closed behind us. "I don't know what's up with her lately."

"What's wrong?"

"For the past month or two, she hasn't been herself," Serafine told me. "Gone all the time. We started this whole thing as a partnership, but lately, I'm wondering if maybe the old advice about mixing business and family was something I should have paid more attention to."

"What do you think is going on?" I asked as we walked away from the house toward the back of the property.

"I don't know, but I wish she'd get past it," she said. "It's hard enough trying to keep the place going with two people; solo, it's next to impossible."

"I hear you," I said. "Some days I'd love it if someone else would get up and milk the cow and do the chores."

"Not a lot of vacation days for a farmer, are there?" Serafine asked as we approached the nearest hive.

"No, not so much," I said. "Hey, did Rooster ask you any more questions about what happened to Bug Wharton the other night?"

I felt the atmosphere change, and her response was clipped. "No. Why?"

"Oh... He can be a total idiot, that's all."

Her tone turned sharp. "I heard some people in town think I cast a spell on him, or poisoned him, or something."

"Anytime something happens, the rumor mill starts

going. People talk," I said, "but it doesn't mean anything. Honestly, I'm more worried about Rooster than anyone else. He doesn't like outsiders."

"Or witches or people of color, either, I imagine." Her voice was bitter.

I wasn't going to argue with her on that one; she was probably right. "Let's just take it a day at a time, Serafine. I believe in what you're doing here. You know you can count me as a friend."

A small smile brightened her face. "Thanks. I'm sorry I overreacted. Most of the time I'm okay with it, but sometimes... well, sometimes it gets to me."

"I imagine so," I said. "And last night was kind of a nightmare."

"Kind of?" She gave a wry laugh. "I keep handing things over to the goddess, trying not to worry about things I can't control, but some days it's hard."

"I hear you," I said, thinking about my unsolved well problem as we approached the hives.

"But enough about that," she said. "Let's talk about bees."

She spent the next half hour introducing me to bee-keeping and showing me how to set up a hive. When I left, it was with a block of beeswax and a chunk of honeycomb.

I gave her a big hug; she smelled like spices and honey. "Thanks, Serafine."

She grinned at me. "Happy to help. I'll e-mail you the hive info tonight."

"I'll look for it." I hesitated. "Have you thought about having a rain date for the Witches' Ball, by the way? Halloween is next Saturday; Friday the thirtieth would be perfect."

"I'll think about it," she said. "In the meantime,

thanks for all your support." She squeezed my hand and I thanked her again for the tour—and the goodies.

As I pulled out of the Honeyed Moon winery, I noticed a beat-up green Kia near the entrance, with a "Keep Austin Weird" sticker on the back. It looked awfully familiar.

With a sinking feeling, I realized it was the same car I'd seen at the exotic game ranch earlier that day.

Chapter 6

PETER STILL WASN'T HOME WHEN I left the winery, so I left a voicemail on his cell and headed home, where I spent the remainder of the afternoon in my kitchen. After making it through a long, blistering summer, the cool weather of autumn always left me wanting to bake. Using some leftover chicken I had in the fridge, I put together a chicken pot pie for dinner later with Quinn, Peter, and Tobias, making extra pie dough so I could whip up a batch of my grandmother's apple dumplings. Once the pie was ready to go, I tucked it into the fridge and checked to make sure I had everything ready for the Sunday afternoon market—it was delayed a day because of a high school event—and then retrieved my grandmother's cookbook from the top of the pie safe, turning to her apple dumpling recipe. I knew Quinn would be bringing pie, but I'd been thinking about those dumplings all week. Some of my fondest memories were of baking in the kitchen with her, and the way the week had gone, I was in need of some comfort.

Once I found the recipe, I started coring and peeling six of the apples I'd picked up at the market on the square the previous week.

When I'd finished preparing the apples, I took the pie dough left over from the pot pie out of the fridge—I'd made a double batch—and rolled it out on the piece of marble I kept for such occasions, then cut it into six squares.

As I distributed the cored apples among the dough squares, my thoughts turned to Aimee. Serafine had said she'd been acting strange the last couple of months; I was guessing I knew why. How long had she and Mitch been seeing each other? I wondered as I cut up a stick of butter and tucked pieces into the apples, then loaded the tops and the sides with brown sugar, cinnamon, and nutmeg.

Aimee had obviously broken up with Mitch. Had he killed his brother to be able to provide for her better… and maybe keep her from calling things off? I sprayed a baking dish with cooking spray, moistened my fingers, and began gathering the corners of the pie dough squares and making the dumplings. What did he have that she wanted back? And why wouldn't he give it to her?

When the unbaked dumplings were arranged in the baking pan, I added water, sugar, vanilla, and the rest of the butter to a saucepan on the stove and turned on the burner, inhaling the sweet aroma as I stirred it. I could practically taste the spicy, buttery sweetness of the dumplings, with their flaky crust and their soft apple insides; just the thought of it brought up warm memories of my grandmother, whose presence I always felt in the farmhouse. It was like having my own personal guardian angel. "I miss you, Grandma," I said out loud. I didn't know if she could hear me, but I wanted her to know.

Chuck was more concerned with the food itself than nostalgia. He hadn't left my side since I started cooking, and kept cocking his head and looking up at me with sad brown eyes. I took pity on him and tossed him a chunk of apple and a leftover scrap of pie dough. He devoured them in an instant and looked up at me, wanting more. I gave him the last little scrap of pie dough and cleaned up the kitchen as the scent of apple dumplings filled the little house.

As I wiped down the marble slab, my thoughts turned to Teena Marburger and her proclamation of death. The reading had been for Peter. Was what happened to Bug linked to Peter, somehow? Or was she referring to something else that hadn't happened yet... and that might involve the young farmer?

Although I hadn't known Bug very well, and wasn't what you'd call close, I had a bad feeling about what was to come. Would whoever killed Bug Wharton stop at one death? Or would there be another victim soon?

Peter and Quinn came over at six, bearing a pecan pie and a six-pack of Shiner Oktoberfest beer.

"Come on in," I said, and Chuck just about did a somersault trying to jump all over Pip, who had bounded in after Quinn. Quinn had adopted Pip at the beginning of the summer, and the formerly small black puppy was turning out to be a rather enormous, but very sweet, Lab mix. Quinn brought her out to the farm every time she came; there wasn't a lot of room to run around in her apartment over the Blue Onion, and Pip usually enticed Chuck into some much-needed exercise.

Once we'd shooed the dogs out into the yard, where Pip immediately started investigating the perimeter for signs of squirrels, we headed into the kitchen. Peter opened beers for us as Quinn offered to help me finish dinner prep.

"I pretty much took care of everything this afternoon. You can help with the dishes," I told her as I poked a few holes in the top of the chicken pot pie I'd prepared to vent it. "I just have to slip this into the oven and dress the salad, and we're ready to go."

"Where's Tobias?" Peter asked as he sat down at the table.

"He's still taking care of an oryx we found at the Safari Exotic Game Ranch," I told him. "He's going to be a few minutes late."

"What happened?" Peter asked.

"It was attacked. He thinks it might have been a mountain lion," I told him.

"Mountain lion? That's serious business," Peter said. "When did this happen?"

"We found her today," I said.

"The ranch isn't too far from my place. I'd better make sure everyone's locked up safe tonight."

"They're not the only one having problems," Quinn said. "Myrtle Crenshaw was at the cafe this afternoon talking about how a chupacabra left a deer in bad shape in her backyard."

"A chupacabra?"

"She says she saw it skulking away," she said.

"I doubt that," Peter said. "Probably a coyote. I've heard a few packs out here... none recently, but there are some in the area. Still," he said, "I'll watch out for the girls. Sometimes I think I should get a guard dog, but I don't think I could bear to leave it outside all night."

"Chuck does a pretty good job from the foot of the bed," I said. Quinn and I exchanged glances; we both remembered how he had tried to protect her from her violent ex one night.

"He's out of jail, you know," Quinn said quietly.

"What?"

"He got out on parole last week," she said. After assaulting Quinn in my kitchen, Jed Stadtler been sentenced to time in jail. I'd hoped he'd be out of commission for a good long time, but evidently, I was out of luck.

"Have you heard from him?" I asked as I slid the pot pie into the oven.

"Not yet," she said ominously, and Peter reached over and grasped her hand.

"You know you can always stay here," I told her.

"As much as I appreciate the offer, I hate the thought of changing anything in my life just because of that jerk," she replied, running a hand through her red curls. Her voice was defiant, but her movements were jerky.

"I understand, but the door is always open. Besides, I'd love the company. And I know Chuck would, too."

"Thanks for the offer," she said. "I'll think about it."

"You know the door's open at my place, too," Peter reminded her.

"I know," she said with a tired smile. "Thank you both. It means so much to me."

Just then, there was a knock on the front door, followed by a hearty "Hello!" from Tobias.

"Come in!" I called, and a moment later he walked into the kitchen with a bouquet of yellow wildflowers and a weary-looking smile.

"For you," he announced.

"Thanks." I kissed him and reached for a Mason jar as Peter offered him a beer.

"What's this I hear about a mountain lion?" Peter

asked when we'd all settled in at the table, the Mason jar of cheery wildflowers in the center.

"That's my best guess as to what went after the oryx Lucy and I found today," Tobias said.

"Quinn said someone was talking about a chupacabra," I said.

"I heard about that," Tobias said. "The deer in the pasture, right?"

Quinn nodded. "What do you think?"

"I think something's out there," Tobias said. "But it's hard to tell what. Like I said, my best guess is a mountain lion. I took some photos and sent them to a friend of mine from vet school. We'll see what he thinks."

"It's been an exciting couple of days," I said, and turned to Tobias. "Guess who was at the game ranch at the same time we were?"

"Who?" he asked.

"Aimee Alexandre," I told him.

"Wait a moment. She was the one we heard talking to Mitch?"

"I don't know," I said, "but I saw a green Kia that looked a lot like hers at Honeyed Moon when I swung by to ask about bees this afternoon."

"Has Serafine heard anything else from Rooster?" Tobias asked.

"Not as of this afternoon," I replied. "Something tells me we haven't heard the last of it, though."

"And I still can't get over that death card thing," Peter said.

"Me neither," I admitted.

Quinn shuddered. "Creepy. I was thinking about Teena today, by the way. I think you should have her check out your new house. If it's haunted, she'll be able to tell you."

"That's just what I need," I said. "Ghost confirmation."

"It could be a selling point," Quinn said. "You could do ghost-hunter weekends."

"Assuming it doesn't fall in on them," I pointed out.

"We'll take a look at that tonight," Peter said.

"Actually, what I need even sooner is to get my well taken care of. I still haven't heard any action plan from Lenny."

"What are you doing for water?" Peter asked.

"I don't know yet," I said. "Any way I could get the pumper truck to deliver some water to tide me over?"

"I can't think why not," Peter said. "I'll ask down at the station, but that's only a short-term fix. What's going on?"

"I was hoping it might be that the pump needed to be lowered, but Lenny told me I need to drill a new well. Unfortunately, the local dowser passed away recently, and Lenny doesn't seem to have another way of locating water." I took a swig of beer. "I was hoping we might get a tropical depression to park over Buttercup and get the well back up and running, but there's no rain in the forecast." Hurricanes and tropical depressions, while devastating to the coastal cities, were an important source of water for the rest of Texas. We always prayed that big gulf storms were mild, slow-moving, missed the population centers, and parked over Fayette County, refilling the aquifer. Texas was, as a friend once put it, "perpetual drought interrupted by intermittent flooding."

"Not good," Quinn said.

"Exactly. I've got to come up with a plan, and soon. Quinn grimaced. "It's always something, isn't it?"

"Do you think Teena can magically find water?"

Peter suggested, only half-joking. "She seems to be able to predict everything else."

An uneasy silence descended on the table as we all thought of Bug Wharton's untimely death. And Peter's altercation with the man just before he died.

"She should market her skills. Haunted house evaluation, water location... she could open an online psychic service," I said. "She really pegged it at the winery the other night. It was spooky."

"Speaking of the other night, have you seen Rooster since the Witches' Ball?" Tobias asked Quinn.

She shook her head. "Thank goodness," she said. "I'm hoping they rule his death an accident."

"It was a bee sting," I said. "What else could it be?"

"I've never had an EpiPen fail before," Tobias said. "I did some research online; there haven't been any recent recalls."

"Maybe we got it to him too late," I said, reaching out to touch his hand. "There was nothing you could do."

"I know," he replied, taking a swig of his beer. "It just bothers me."

"How long till dinner?" Quinn asked brightly, obviously attempting to change the subject.

"Twenty minutes," I said, checking the timer.

"Well, then. Let's go check out your haunted house!"

Chapter 7

"I'M NOT SURE I'D SAY it's haunted," I demurred, not liking the idea of having transported a haunted house to Dewberry Farm. Of course, there had been enough strange coincidences since I moved to the farm that I was pretty sure my grandmother was still watching over me, but she was a friendly ghost, so to speak. "Maybe you all can tell me what I need to do to it to make it habitable," I suggested. "Or at least keep it from caving in on itself."

Together, we stepped out into the cool night air. Now that it was October, while most days weren't what I'd call nippy, the evenings were delightful, and tonight was almost cool enough to entice me to start a fire in the woodstove. I unwound the sweater from my waist and pulled it on over my head as we headed through the kissing gate and walked down the path to the old house. Pip bounded up to us, followed a moment later by a panting Chuck.

"He's getting his exercise, isn't he?" Tobias said approvingly as he put an arm around my shoulders and gave me a squeeze. "No extra treats?"

"I can't promise that," I said, thinking guiltily of the pie crust I'd slipped him earlier that day, "but I'm trying."

In the fading evening light, the little wood house

seemed desolate, as if it knew it had been abandoned. The front porch slewed to the left, and I felt another pang of buyer's remorse. I was glad I'd been able to save the old building from destruction, but I wasn't sure I was going to be able to afford to fix it up it before it fell over.

"This is a perfect site for it," Peter said. "It's a sweet little house."

"Think it'll fall over if we go into it? Quinn asked, echoing my fears.

"Have you been in it since they moved it?" Peter asked me.

"I have," I said. "A few of the floorboards are a bit springy, but it didn't fall in on me."

"I'll take a look," Peter told us. "I used to help renovate houses in the summers."

"I'll come with you," Tobias said. Peter stepped up onto the porch gingerly and opened the front door. Tobias followed a moment later, and we could hear the boards squeaking as he walked around the first floor.

"Did Maria tell you all about how the place is supposed to be haunted?" Quinn asked.

Just the thought of it put an eerie cast on the house, somehow. "She told me Indians killed one of her ancestors and abducted his daughter," I said.

"That's it," she said.

"What's the story?" Tobias asked.

"There was a Comanche raid one night. The wife was in Galveston with several of the children, visiting relatives; it was just the father and his teenage daughter who were home. He died and she disappeared; they found him on the front porch."

Maria hadn't told me that detail. I looked at the leaning porch, trying to imagine the scene. "That's horrible.

No one ever heard from her again, right?"

Quinn shook her head. "I don't know, but eventually another family ended up with the house, though they didn't stay long. There have been stories about it ever since."

"Like what?"

"You know. Weird noises, the sound of a woman screaming..."

"I can't think why they didn't stay," I said dryly.

"Have you heard anything weird?" Quinn asked.

"No. But I haven't exactly spent a lot of time down here," I admitted. And nor, now, would I want to, necessarily. I'd wanted to rent it out as a guesthouse, but I wondered how guests would take to ghostly women screaming and banging in the middle of the night. "It's been busy, and I've been worried about the whole water situation." I glanced over and surveyed my gardens; so far, things still looked okay, but I was going to have to solve my water problem soon, or everything I was growing would die. And without any produce from the farm, I was toast. My mortgage wasn't huge, but it still needed to be paid. Thank goodness the animals still had a good bit of water in their troughs. I stifled a sigh; I couldn't do anything about it right now anyway, so there was no use in worrying tonight.

"I think it's sound," Peter called out. "A few soft floorboards, and I wouldn't use the stairs just yet, but I think you're safe."

"Shall we?" Quinn asked.

"Sure," I said and followed her up onto the porch and into the front door. As I stepped inside, there was a whining noise behind me; Chuck and Pip were standing at the base of the porch steps. "We'll be right out," I reassured them, but it didn't help. The whining just increased.

"This place has a lot of potential," Quinn breathed in as she looked around. The floors were wide planks of pine, and the walls were painted wood boards. Although they were dingy, they had been painted white, with a beautiful blue stencil pattern along the top of the wall. "This could be a great living room, and you could put the kitchen and a nice eating table at the end, and there's room for a bathroom maybe under the stairs. The windows are terrific," she said. My mind started totting up the expenses as she spoke.

Peter ran a finger along the window frame. "The windows have wood rot."

"But they've got that lovely wavy glass," Quinn said. "The light in here must be just fantastic. What's upstairs?"

"One long room that could be broken up into two bedrooms," I said. Before moving the house, I'd taken a peek, and in a moment of insanity, had said, "I love the windows at the ends of the house; they're triple windows, and I kind of envision hanging stained glass in the middle window." Even now, the thought of it made me a little excited, and I found myself thinking about how beautiful the floors would be if they were refinished. I looked up at the stenciling and wondered about the woman who had painted it. What dreams had she had? And how had she felt when she came home to discover her husband dead and her daughter missing? There was tragedy everywhere, I sometimes thought, even in beautiful things.

She might be gone, but I wanted to preserve her handiwork. Once I got the water situation figured out, I decided, I'd come down and wash down the walls, and at least sweep the place out. Maybe we could sweep out the sadness and bring new life to it. With a few rosebushes by the front porch, a fresh coat of paint, and an old-fashioned range in the little kitchen... I was already picturing a Mason jar filled with wildflowers on a round wooden table...

Bang.

I felt my heart jump in my chest.

"What was that?" Quinn hissed.

Tobias was eyeing the ceiling. "It came from upstairs."

A moment later the wind kicked up, shaking some of the windows, and there was a low, moaning sound. The dogs started barking madly.

Bang. Bang. It sounded like someone hammering a frying pan.

"I'm getting out of here," Quinn said, making a bee-line for the door. I followed her; when we got outside, the dogs were whining nervously. They jumped all over Quinn, and then me, as if making sure we were okay.

Peter came out a moment later, but Tobias lingered for a moment before stepping onto the porch in a lei-surely fashion.

"What took you so long?" I asked as he joined us in front of the house.

"I was trying to figure out what was making that noise," he told me.

"It was creepy," Quinn said, shivering. "Maybe we need to get Teena out here to look around. She seems to have a direct line to the other side, if you know what I mean." Our collective thoughts turned to Bug Wharton again.

"The pot pie's probably almost done," I said. "We should probably head back."

"Probably," Peter said, still squinting at the house. "Bang or no bang, the house has good bones and lots of history," he told me. "If you need help, I'm happy to give you a hand with the renovation."

"Thanks," I said. "Once I get my water situation taken care of, I may take you up on that." We stood and listened for a few minutes longer, but the only sound was the wind soughing through the grass. The temperature had dropped while we were in the house; I shivered.

"What do you think that noise was?" Quinn asked in a quiet voice.

"Probably something loose upstairs," he said. "The wind must have been knocking something around."

"But all the windows are closed," I pointed out.

"I'm sure there's a rational explanation," Tobias said. "But what I'm more worried about," he continued as he put his arm around me and we turned back toward the farmhouse, "is what we're going to do about your animals."

"Me too," I said. "If we can't get the pumper truck out to fill the stock tank, I'm in trouble."

"If you can't get it worked out, why don't you bring them over to my place until you get things squared away?" Peter asked. "You can come over and help me milk everybody."

"I hate to move them, but that would be great. Are you sure?" I asked.

"Sure. I miss Gidget and Hot Lips, and I'm sure Blossom and Peony would enjoy the company. It'll be like a minigetaway for them. Visiting cousins."

I laughed. "Actually, that would solve a big part of my problem," I said. "If you're sure."

"I'm positive," he said. "I'll bring the trailer over tomorrow, and we'll get them loaded up."

"Thank you," I said, almost forgetting about the

ominous noises from the old house and feeling much lighter as we approached my grandmother's yellow farmhouse.

"If we fill the stock tanks, can you use them to water your vegetables?" Quinn asked.

"I sure hope so," I said, surveying my pumpkin patch, which was just about ready to be harvested and turned into pumpkin butter. It was a good thing I had some big pots to make it with; I just hoped the rest sold at market.

"How much do you think filling the stock tanks would run her?" Tobias asked Peter.

"I told Lucy I'd ask about it tomorrow," Peter said. "I'm sure we can get you the friends and family discount, anyway," he added with a wink.

"And I'll ask around for a dowser," Quinn said. "There's got to be a water witch around somewhere."

"Water witch," I said. "What about Serafine? She's a witch."

"Is she?" Tobias asked. "I thought those went extinct in the seventeen hundreds."

"She and her sister are Wiccan," I said.

"What does that mean?" Quinn asked.

"They worship what they call the horned god and goddess," Peter supplied, "and the turning of the seasons, or the wheel of the year." Peter was from Austin, which—aside from the legislature—was the counterculture epicenter of Texas, and he was pretty up on all kinds of things you usually didn't find in small-town Texas.

"Sounds intriguing," I said as we stepped into the pot-pie-scented farmhouse. "I don't know how that relates to finding water, but it's worth asking." Besides, I was curious about Aimee and Mitch; I was hoping I could ask her a few questions.

"The pot pie smells delicious," Quinn said as we all gathered around the kitchen table. Tobias replenished everyone's beers, and I had just finished dressing the salad when the timer buzzed. The pot pie was a gorgeous golden brown, with bits of golden filling bubbling up around the edges.

"And looks amazing," Tobias said as I put it down on the table.

"I'm usually vegetarian," Peter said, "but I make an exception for an occasional pastured-chicken pot pie."

"It's not one of mine," I confessed. "I got it from another farmer at the market." I may have been an investigative reporter in my former life, and I knew my grandmother had been less than sentimental about her animals—with the exception of her favorite cow, Gertrude—but I couldn't bring myself to eat an animal I had gotten to know personally.

"Cheers," I said as I sat down and raised my glass, thankful for the wonderful people around the table with me. We'd all just clinked glasses and were about to dig in when Pip and Chuck started barking wildly from the yard.

"Who's that?" Quinn asked, squinting out the wavy front window.

"Looks like a police cruiser," Tobias said in a grim voice.

"If it's Rooster, I'd better go corral Chuck."

"That's right," Tobias said with a wry grin. "He took a chunk out of Rooster's pants a while back, didn't he?"

I headed toward the front door and called Chuck, who was growling menacingly at our local sheriff. Rooster had stepped out of his Crown Victoria and was eyeing Chuck with suspicion.

"What can we help you with?" I asked once I had Chuck's collar firmly in hand.

"Wanted to talk to Peter and Tobias," he said. "Heard I could find y'all here."

"About what?" Tobias asked.

"About what happened out at that witch's place, at the ball."

My eyebrows shot up, and Quinn and I glanced at each other.

"You mean what happened with Bug Wharton and the anaphylactic shock?" Tobias asked.

"If that's what it was," he said.

I led Chuck to the front door and shooed him inside. Pip followed without being asked. Only when Chuck was safely inside did Rooster squeeze through the gate and into my front yard.

"We were just about to sit down to dinner, actually," Tobias told him.

I smiled and forced myself to be polite. "We were. I just pulled a chicken pot pie out of the oven. Would you like to join us?"

"No, ma'am. This is a business visit, not a pleasure cruise."

"Do you want to talk now, or would you rather we stopped by tomorrow?" Peter asked.

"I'd rather get on with things," he said.

"Did the autopsy results come back, then?" I asked.

"Police business," Rooster said shortly, studying Tobias and Peter. "Which one of you jabbed Bug?"

"I did," Tobias said. "I told you at the time."

"But you handled the thing, too, didn't you?" Rooster asked Peter, adjusting his collar as he spoke. His reddish wattle spilled over the too-tight polyester shirt.

"The EpiPen? I got it out of the glove compartment, yes," Peter said.

"Was there something wrong with the EpiPen, then?" Tobias asked. "Or was it not anaphylaxis?"

"Oh, it was anaphylaxis all right," Rooster said.

"Then why are you questioning Tobias and Peter?" I asked. "If Bug Wharton died of natural causes?"

"I didn't say it was natural," Rooster said. "What made you two decide he needed to be jabbed with an EpiPen?"

"He asked for it, for starters," Tobias pointed out. "And he was exhibiting all the signs of anaphylaxis. It all happened fast; you don't have much time to think in a situation like that."

"I heard he had a dustup with Serafine Alexandre," Rooster said.

"They argued, yes."

"From what I hear, she threatened to kill him," Rooster said. "And then she gave him a drink of that mead stuff."

"She did," I confirmed, "but it came from the same place as everyone else's drink."

"If she knew he was allergic to bees, that would be an easy way to kill someone off. Giving them honey wine," Rooster said.

"Being allergic to bee venom doesn't mean you're allergic to honey," Tobias explained. "It's the protein in the venom that people react to. Honey is primarily sugar, and any proteins in it are different from those in the venom."

"Hmm," Rooster said. "It doesn't seem suspicious at all that she threw his cup into the fire afterward? Sounds to me like destroying evidence."

"Just because Serafine argued with Bug doesn't mean

she killed him," I pointed out. "Besides, she didn't
know he was going to come up to her. Everyone was
drinking from that cauldron."

"You and Bug crossed sabers, too," Rooster said,
squinting at Peter. "I hear you weren't a big supporter
of his new ranch."

"That's true," Peter said.

"You wrote a letter to the paper about it not too
long ago. Pretty passionate."

"I did," Peter acknowledged. Quinn shifted from
foot to foot, looking nervous.

"Y'all know anything else about that Serafine
woman? Says she's a witch."

"What does that have to do with what happened to
Bug Wharton?" I asked. "You think she put a spell on
him?"

"I think maybe she put something in that drink she
gave him," Rooster said.

"I noticed a twist of paper with a dead bee in it in
the front seat of his truck," I said, knowing that my
mentioning it would make Rooster far less likely to
investigate it, but unable to stop myself. "And the window was cracked open. Maybe someone who knew he
was allergic to bees put some of them in his truck so
he'd be stung when he got back in."

"Lots of bees around that winery place," Rooster
said. "One of 'em probably flew in through the window and got toasted in the heat."

"It wasn't that hot that evening. Besides," Tobias said,
"it would be worth checking on. There could be fingerprints on the paper."

"I'll mention it to the lab," Rooster said in a dismis-
sive tone that meant he would do no such thing, and
then focused on Tobias again. "You're familiar with

EpiPens, right?"

"I've used EpiPens on animals, yes."

"Was there anything different about the one you used on Bug?"

"Not that I noticed," he said. "It was a little hectic; I wasn't focusing on the details. You, Peter?"

Peter shrugged. "I wouldn't know. It's the first time I've seen one."

"Why are you asking?" Tobias asked. "Was there something wrong with it? I researched, and there haven't been any recalls lately. Is that why he died? A defective syringe?"

"Did any of y'all see that Serafine woman before Bug died?"

"We got there at the same time as Bug did," I said. "Peter had a tarot reading done, and then we went to get some mead. As far as I know, Serafine was serving mead the whole time; we weren't there for very long."

"I heard you had quite a reading," Rooster said. "Got a card that looked just like your costume," he said, nodding at Peter. "I also heard you thought Bug Wharton deserved to be shot."

Peter shifted uncomfortably. "I don't remember what I said, but I know I was upset about the game ranch. It's common knowledge how I feel about animals."

"It sure is," Rooster said. "In the paper and everything. Anyway," Rooster said with a smug smile, "I'll let y'all get back to dinner now. But don't be leavin' town anytime soon. I'll be back." He tipped his hat and opened the gate, leaving the four of us staring after him.

"Does he really think Peter might have killed Bug Wharton?" Quinn asked as we watched Rooster's cruiser bump down my driveway.

"Either Peter or Serafine, sounds like," Tobias said. "He said a lot more than he should have if it's an open case."

"Well," I said, "let's go in and get dinner. I, for one, could use another beer."

"I think we all could," Peter said, and I opened the door to the farmhouse. A moment later we walked into the kitchen, where Pip and Chuck were standing on the table and finishing off the last of the pot pie.

Chapter 8

"PIP! I CAN'T BELIEVE YOU did that!" Quinn gasped. "She's never done anything like that before!"

"I'm afraid Chuck's been a bad influence," I said. As we stared at the dogs, who were licking their lips and looking completely unrepentant, I turned to Tobias. "See what I'm up against?"

He gave me a wry grin as I shooed both dogs off the table and out the door.

"Damn Rooster," Quinn said. "He ruined a perfect evening. And your beautiful pot pie..."

"We've still got salad, at least. Why don't I whip up some pasta? I put lots of tomato sauce up this summer; we'll just heat that up and have a pasta dinner." I glanced over to where the pecan pie sat on the counter, unmolested. "Besides, at least they didn't get to the pie. Or the apple dumplings." I'd left the dumplings in the pie safe, thankfully.

"Good thing," Tobias said. "I might have to pump their stomachs; pecans aren't good for dogs."

"I learn something new every day," I told Tobias.

As Tobias filled a pasta pot with water, and Peter and Quinn helped me clean up what the dogs hadn't gotten to, the conversation turned to Rooster.

"Why on earth did he see the need to come out here

after-hours?" Quinn asked. "Just to ruin our dinner?"

"It wouldn't surprise me," I said as I wiped up another smear of gravy. "It sounds like something was up with that EpiPen, that's for sure."

"I'm wondering if it wasn't defective," Tobias said. "It's been known to happen."

"And I'm wondering if someone tampered with it," I replied. "He sure was treating it like Bug's death was foul play."

"If so, Peter, you'd better watch out," Quinn said. "Everyone in town knows you had it in for Bug."

"He and Serafine weren't on good terms either," Tobias pointed out. "Everyone in town saw the blowup over the cauldron."

"And he died just a few minutes later," Quinn said. "I wish she hadn't tossed that cup into the fire."

Peter finished sweeping up the last of the crumbs. "Well, nobody's been charged yet, so I vote we table it until we have to. I'd rather talk about dealing with Lucy's water problems."

Quinn sighed. "Do you really think the fire department will come out to deliver water?"

"I do," he said. "The problem is, it won't do anything to help the well. Unless the well is dug, it won't hold water. How many stock tanks do you have?"

"Two," I said, "and they're not very big. Plus, I'd need some kind of pump to get the irrigation going."

"Lenny said he was sure it wasn't a problem with the pump?"

"He told me the well had run dry," I replied. "And that I'd either have to drill deeper or put in a new one."

"So much for the quiet, easy small-town life, eh?" Quinn asked with a sidelong grin.

"Exactly," I said, and my mind flitted back to the

threat of Jed Stadtler. Neither of us was having a particularly good week.

As if reading my mind, Peter walked over and squeezed Quinn's shoulders. "Whatever happens, we'll get through it."

"We will," Tobias echoed, looking at me.

Tobias stayed behind once Peter and Quinn had left. Although we'd missed the pot pie, the pasta with homemade sauce was a delicious substitute, and Quinn's pie and my grandmother's apple dumplings made for a satisfying ending—particularly with a scoop of Blue Bell Homemade Vanilla Ice Cream.

While Tobias finished drying the last of the plates, I brewed a pot of decaf. When the last plate was put up, we took two mugs out onto the front porch and sat down in the rocking chairs together, looking up at the stars.

"I have a bad feeling about all this," I told him as he reached out to squeeze my hand.

"I didn't want to say anything to Peter, but I do, too," he replied. "Rooster looks like he's trying to narrow down his suspect list."

I sipped my warm coffee and shivered, despite my heavy sweater. "I may need to check in with Opal at the station or call Mandy down at the Zephyr to see if they've heard anything about the autopsy report."

"I keep wondering what the connection is between Aimee and Mitch Wharton," Tobias commented. "Do you think they were seeing each other on the sly?"

"I'm guessing they were, and if I'm right, I'm sure someone at the ranch knows about it. But if Bug was murdered, what would that have to do with it?"

"I don't know who owns the majority share of the ranch," Tobias said. "Or who gets it in the event of a death. Did Bug have any kids?"

"Not that I know of, but that doesn't mean he didn't."

"The ranch is an expensive piece of property," Tobias said. "It sold for a couple million."

"That's a lot of down payment to come up with."

"They paid for it in cash, actually."

I let out a long, low whistle. "Where'd they get that? A relative in the oil business?"

Tobias took a long sip of his coffee. "I don't think so. They never talked much about what they did, only that it was something in tech."

"A start-up that did an IPO, maybe?" I mused.

"It's worth checking out. If it is considered homicide, that is."

"Lord knows Rooster isn't going to do much in the way of investigating."

"Well, let's hope it doesn't come to that," I said. "That way, I can focus on my water problems and my falling-down haunted house instead."

"I'm sure it isn't haunted," Tobias objected.

"Oh, really? What was that banging sound, then?"

"A loose shutter or something."

"There aren't any shutters."

"Okay, a loose something. Once we can get up to the second floor, we'll figure it out. Did you know there was a house just outside of town that was supposed to be haunted? Footsteps on the roof every night."

"On the roof?"

"Exactly. Turned out the goats were escaping their pen and climbing up on the roof to get to the pear tree growing right next to the house."

I burst out laughing. "Really?"

"Really," he said. "They locked themselves back in their pen before morning."

"They're smart little buggers, aren't they?"

"Speaking of smart little buggers, yours have been remarkably well-behaved lately. I haven't gotten a single phone call about livestock chowing down on the geraniums in the Square."

"Don't jinx me," I warned him. Blossom, my first cow, had, unbeknownst to me, been known as Harriet Houdini before I acquired her, and my goats, Hot Lips and Gidget, were talented escape artists as well. Now that everyone had offspring, maybe they would be too worried about their babies to give in to wanderlust. Time would tell.

"I don't mean to pressure you," Tobias said, "but you really need to get that well sorted out. It's supposed to be a La Niña winter."

I groaned. "That means no rain, right?"

"Exactly. No relief in sight." Droughts in Texas, always a problem, seemed to be more and more of an issue the past several years. "It's tough on farmers and ranchers. A lot of folks will be selling their livestock."

"I don't want to be one of them," I said. "But even if it does start raining, I'm going to reach carrying capacity here pretty soon, with everyone calving and kidding every year."

"You might have to think about selling some of your animals," he suggested.

"I hate to do it." One of the things I loved about the farm was that I could keep my little animal families together. At least so far, anyway. "For now," I told him, "I'm going to limit my concerns to water. I hope Peter's right about the fire station being able to deliver some, but I don't know how I'm going to use it to irrigate the crops."

"A pump and a few hoses should take care of it. You'll get it worked out," Tobias said. "You live in Buttercup now; your neighbors aren't going to let you fail."

"Really?"

"Really." He squeezed my hand again. "And your neighbors aren't the only ones."

Not for the first time, despite the problems looming over Dewberry Farm, I felt a surge of gratitude for the new life I'd made for myself. Tobias put down his coffee and stood up, still holding onto my hand. He pulled me up out of my rocking chair and into an embrace. His lips had just met mine when a strong wind came up from the direction of the pasture, and there was a loud bang from the direction of the old house. The goats bleated in alarm, and Tobias and I jumped.

"What the heck was that?" I asked.

"I don't know, but I'm going to check it out," Tobias said. I pulled my sweater tight around me and followed him out the gate toward the house.

"Do you think it's going to fall down?" I asked. "It sounded kind of like timbers cracking, don't you think?"

"It did, but I'm trying not to jump to any conclusions."

Together, we walked down to the house. By the time we got there, the hair was standing up all over my body; it sounded more like a construction site than a house.

"What do you think it is?"

"I don't know," Tobias said as we walked around the house. "It is kind of creepy, though, isn't it?"

"It is," I concurred. "In fact, I think I don't want to be here anymore."

"You know," he said slowly, "I don't think I do, either. Not that I'm superstitious generally, but..."

Another series of bangs interrupted him.

"Let's go," I said, and we hightailed it back to the house.

The next morning dawned cold and clear, with a light breeze from the north, but none of the rain that often accompanied fronts. Tobias had stayed until the banging ended last night, then left reluctantly, only after I assured him that I'd call if it started up again. Now, I tried not to fret as I made coffee with bottled water—we'd eaten off paper plates the night before to save on water—and left another message for Lenny Froehlich. If I didn't hear back soon, I planned to drive out and sit in his office until I had some answers.

As Chuck watered my grandmother's rosebushes, my eyes were drawn to the Ulrich house.

In the daytime, all the eeriness I had seen last night was gone. It was just a run-down old house with a rotting porch. Cute, but a lot of work. I squinted at it, looking for signs of something flapping loose in the wind, but there was nothing. In the spring, I thought, it would be a lovely place to stay, particularly with the sound of Dewberry Creek burbling in the background. Not that there was any water in the rocky creek bed now; after a reasonably rainy spring, the rush of water had dried to a trickle and then disappeared altogether. We'd had almost no rain to speak of in almost five months.

I turned my attention to my rather limp rows of broccoli. The only saving grace of my water shortage was that I hadn't planted all my fall crops yet, so there wasn't as much to water. That would change soon, though. I'd hoped to sow more lettuce during the next waxing moon; I was starting to experiment with a few old wives' tales to help boost production.

Chuck followed me back into the farmhouse, sniffing hopefully at the fridge door as I grabbed the clean milk pails and headed out to milk everyone. Blossom and Peony were anxiously awaiting me, and the goats were bleating with impatience. The milking went smoothly; I'd started to get the hang of it, and what once took hours was now a relatively straightforward routine. Although Blossom and I had duked it out at the beginning, she'd finally accepted that I was the one in charge, and now was content to munch on her treats while I did my job.

Once the milk had been safely stowed in the fridge, I gathered the few eggs the girls had laid for me and replenished the feeders. I spent the rest of the morning filling buckets from the goats' dwindling stock tank—I hadn't gotten a pump and hose setup put together yet—and lugging them over to my broccoli seedlings. It wasn't the most glamorous work, but as I set down the bucket for the last time and looked out over the golden hills around me, I felt a sense of satisfaction. Even in drought, the land was beautiful... although I had to admit I longed for the verdant green that carpeted the hills after the winter rains. Not that there were going to be any this year, most likely. My stomach tightened and I tried the whole don't-worry-about-what-you-can't-control thing, but it was hard when your livelihood depended on something so unpredictable. Maybe my mother had been right about me buying the farm; she'd thought I was crazy, and there were days when I agreed with her. On the other hand, with newspapers folding left and right, my journalism career hadn't exactly been rock solid, either.

Gidget bleated at me as I put the bucket down next to the stock tank and walked back toward the house. I had friends who would help me out, I had enough eggs to cook up an omelet for lunch, there was a loaf of bread from the Blue Onion Cafe in my cozy kitchen, and Tobias had promised me my neighbors wouldn't let me fail. And maybe the well company had called with a magical solution while I was doing the chores.

But I couldn't worry about that now. The market on the Square started in half an hour. I loaded my wares into the back of my truck and headed into town, trying to leave my troubles behind.

The market went pretty well, all things considered; the crowd was a bit smaller because of the time change, but the folks who showed up were happy to buy. Although I was short on greens, I sold lots of candles and just about cleared out my stock of pumpkin butter; I was going to have to make a big batch before next week's market. There was lots of buzz about Bug Wharton, and more about whatever was stalking Buttercup's livestock, but I didn't find out anything I didn't already know.

As I pulled up the driveway to the farmhouse, I found myself hoping there would be some news on the well situation. Unfortunately, no messages awaited me when I got back into the kitchen. I washed my hands at the sink and decided I'd figure out what to do after a snack, trying to find comfort in my cozy kitchen.

I had just cracked three eggs into a bowl—one was for Chuck, who loved eggs—and was still consoling myself with Tobias's encouraging words when I heard the sound of tires crunching on my long dirt driveway.

Chuck perked up, growling as menacingly as a chubby poodle can, and together we walked to the front door. I was hoping it might be a pumper truck with water for my stock tanks—or maybe Lenny, my disappearing well consultant—but it was neither.

"What's wrong?" I asked as Aimee threw open the front door of her Kia.

"Serafine's been arrested," she said, looking ashen. "Rooster just turned up and took her to jail!"

Chapter 9

IT WASN'T UNTIL I HAD her sitting at my kitchen table with a mug of coffee that I got anything else out of Aimee.

"Rooster showed up this morning," she blurted out. "Told her she was under arrest for the murder of Bug Wharton."

So, it was homicide after all, I thought. At least Rooster thought so.

"Did he say why he thought it was your sister?"

"I think it was that cup she threw in the fire," Aimee told me, gripping her mug like it was a life preserver. "He said something about destroying evidence."

"Did she say anything when he arrested her?"

Aimee shook her head. "She just let him handcuff her and take her outside and put her in the back of the car." There were tears in her eyes.

"She needs an attorney," I said. "Do you know if she's got one?"

Aimee shook her head. "I'm sure she doesn't. We never needed one before."

"I know a good one in Houston," I said. "Serafine needs to not talk to anyone until she's got a lawyer with her."

My well troubles forgotten, I picked up the phone. A few minutes later, my old friend Andrea Morton had agreed to talk to Serafine. "Let's head down to the station and give her Andrea's number," I told Aimee. Together, we piled into my truck—Aimee's Kia had too much junk in the front seat for me to fit—and headed toward town.

Aimee dabbed at her almond-shaped eyes as I drove, and I couldn't help thinking about her rather heated discussion with Mitch Wharton. "How well do you know the Whartons?" I asked.

She darted a glance at me, then out her window. "Not really at all," she lied. "Why?"

"I'm wondering why Rooster might think your sister had something to do with Bug's death," I told her.

"Well, of course it was because they argued at the Witches' Ball!" she said.

"No other reason?" I prodded.

She dismissed the idea with a toss of her head. "Of course not." I didn't press. At least not yet.

Opal Gruber was seated behind the front desk of the station when we walked in a few minutes later, her short blond hair a bouffant around her round face.

"Oh, you poor dear," she cooed as soon as she spotted Aimee. Opal had been a little chilly to me at first, but she and I had become friendly over the last year. "I'm so sorry about your sister, honey."

"Has she talked with Rooster yet, do you know?" I asked.

Opal shook her Aqua-Netted head. "He headed over to the Blue Onion for coffee as soon as he brought her in," she said. "Had a meetin' with Mayor Nieder-berger."

For possibly the first time since moving to Butter-cup, I praised Rooster's incompetence. "Can we see her?" I asked. "I got her the name of an attorney."

Opal bit her lip and glanced out the window. She had been my ally in the sheriff's office for the last several months; without her steady presence at the helm, I was pretty sure the entire police force of Buttercup would fall apart. "I suppose so, but be quick. I don't know how long he'll be gone. And for heaven's sake, don't tell anyone!"

"Of course not."

We hurried to the small cell at the back of the station. Serafine was sitting on the twin bed in the corner, leafing through a Texas Monthly magazine. There was a Flying Geese quilt on the bed, and lace curtains almost obscured the bars on the window. Opal liked to keep the place homey.

Serafine stood up as Opal unlocked the cell door. "Aimee! And Lucy! What are you doing here?"

"I knew Lucy had helped other people before, so she was the only person I could think to bring," Aimee blurted out. She hurled herself into her sister's arms, all signs of the conflict I'd seen the day before vanished. "Are you okay?"

"I'm fine," Serafine said, but it was obvious she wasn't. Her normally glowing skin was ashen and the nails on her fingers were ragged. It looked as if she'd been biting them.

"Why did he arrest you?" I asked.

She shrugged. "I don't know."

I sighed. "Do you have an attorney?"

"No." Serafine shook her head. "I never needed one before."

"I called a friend of mine in Houston," I told her. "She's willing to come up and meet with you."

"Do you really think it's going to come to that?" Serafine asked.

"Rooster arrested you for murder," I reminded her, looking to Opal, who confirmed what I'd said with a grim nod. "He's not exactly the most thorough investigator on the planet."

"Or the sharpest knife in the drawer," Opal added. "Don't tell him I said so, though."

"Of course not," Serafine said.

"Did he tell you why he was arresting you?" I asked.

Serafine shook her head. "I'm guessing it must have been because he died right after we had that argument at the Witches' Ball," she said.

"I'll go keep tabs on the front," Opal volunteered, drifting away to give us some privacy.

"Was that the only argument you two had?" I asked. "Or was there something more?"

The two sisters exchanged looks, and a microexpression I couldn't quite decipher flashed over Serafine's face. "No," she said brusquely.

I paused for a moment, waiting to see if she would change her mind, but whatever had flashed between them was closed down. "Well, even if you don't want to tell me," I said, "I'd definitely mention it to the attorney."

"There is one thing..." Aimee began.

"Aimee." Serafine's tone brooked no argument.

"It's nothing," Aimee said, flushing. "I'm sorry I brought it up."

"Okay," I said slowly. "Well, if you change your mind, let me know. I was an investigative reporter in another life, so I might be able to help out."

"Thanks, Lucy." Serafine drew herself up, looking regal. "I know I'm innocent. I'm sure justice will prevail."

I wasn't so sanguine about the course of justice, particularly with Rooster in charge, but Serafine didn't seem interested in my opinion, so I didn't press it. "We should probably run before Rooster gets back, but don't talk to him without an attorney present. Her name is Andrea; I brought you her information." I pressed a piece of paper into her hand. "Have you had your phone call yet?"

She shook her head.

"Well, make this your first one," I said. Aimee gave her sister a big hug; they clung to each other as if they were never going to see each other again.

"Rooster alert!" Opal called from the front.

The sisters broke apart, and Aimee and I hurried to the front of the office, passing Opal as she raced past us with the keys. By the time Rooster swaggered through the front door of the office, we were standing by Opal's desk and she was walking down the hall with a hastily poured cup of coffee.

"Well," he said, surveying us. "Fancy meetin' you here."

Aimee crossed her arms and jutted out her chin. "Why did you arrest my sister?"

"For killin' Bug Wharton," Rooster replied, the red wattle under his chin jiggling as he spoke.

"Why on earth would she kill Bug Wharton?" I asked.

He looked at me as if I were two sandwiches short of a picnic. "Because she's one of those raving-lunatic animal-rights people, far as I can see."

"Not much of a motive," I observed. "There are a lot of ranchers in town."

"They had a personal beef, if that's what you want to call it. Anyway, it's police business."

Behind him, Opal rolled her eyes.

"Now," he continued, hitching his belt up over his prodigious paunch, "unless you've got somethin' else you came down to talk about, some of us have work to do."

"Has she had her phone call yet?" I asked.

He turned to Opal. "Well?"

Opal shook her coiffed head. "Not yet."

"We'll get it taken care of. Now, why don't you ladies go back to knittin', or milkin' goats... or whatever it is you do. Hexin' people and all," he added, narrowing his beady eyes at Aimee.

Aimee drew herself up. "I have never hexed anyone in my entire life, and neither has my sister."

"Right," he said. "It's all voodoo mumbo jumbo anyway, far as I'm concerned."

"Well," I said, watching Aimee's eyes narrow and sensing we were veering into dangerous territory, "We've got to run. We'll be back to check on Serafine later."

"But..." Aimee looked ready to spit bullets.

"Let's go," I said, grabbing her elbow and steering her out the front door.

"That hateful man!" she burst out when the door was safely closed behind us. "I may not have hexed anyone in the past, but I think I'm about to start!"

"Shh!" I said, looking around. Buttercup was for the most part a tolerant town, but there were a few folks who weren't too crazy about the idea of two witches taking up residence within the town lines, and there was no reason to start tongues wagging. It was bad enough Serafine was in jail for killing Bug Wharton. "Let's talk about it in the truck," I said. "I'll take you home."

"I don't want to go home," she complained.

"With Serafine stuck here, somebody's got to take care of things, keep the place going," I reminded her. "Besides, there's nothing else to be done right now. Sometimes doing manual labor can help settle your mind a bit."

"I don't know about that," she said.

As I put the truck into gear, I edged toward the question that had been nagging at me since Tobias and I visited the Safari Exotic Game Ranch. "I heard you and Mitch Wharton talking over at the ranch this week," I said lightly. "I didn't know you two were friends."

Her head snapped around. "What?"

"The day the oryx was attacked," I said. "I heard you two talking, and I saw your car."

"You must be mistaken," she said.

Right. Like there were two green Kias in Buttercup.

"Maybe," I said. "But if you and Serafine have other connections to the Whartons, it could be a problem for Serafine."

"Look," Aimee said,. "Aare you here to help me, or not?"

"I was trained as an investigative reporter," I reminded her. "I believe Serafine is innocent. But I also believe you're not telling me everything. If I don't know the whole story, it's going to be hard for me to figure out what really happened to Bug Wharton."

She pressed her lips tightly together and looked out the window, her arms crossed over her chest. It was so tense in the truck I rolled the window down, as if that would let some of the anger out. As we passed the old train depot, Bessie Mae waved at me, and I waved back, thankful that at least someone was in a good mood—and that there was a little bit of good news in Buttercup. The whole town had taken care of Bessie

Mae for years, making sure she was fed and housed in a little place right by the train station. Her sole joy in life was watching the trains and waving at cars, but a few months ago she had suffered a health crisis that had taken her away from her favorite spot by the train depot. Thanks to the funds raised by the town's Christmas Market, her house on the train station had been renovated so she could manage it in her wheelchair. As I glanced into the rearview mirror, where Bessie Mae was still waving, I made a mental note to bring her a casserole later in the week; it had been a while since I'd stopped by.

Friends looked after each other here in Buttercup, Tobias had told me. I thought of Serafine, locked in a small room with six years of Texas Monthly back issues, and the seething Aimee beside me. I hoped I'd be able to keep both of them from a bad ending.

Unless Aimee told me what was really going on, though, I didn't much like my chances.

I stopped by the Buttercup Veterinary Clinic after I dropped Aimee off at the Honeyed Moon winery; I knew Tobias was there because his truck was out front. The office was empty, but the door was unlocked. I knocked and let myself in.

"Hello!" I called out.

"Lucy? Come on back!" Tobias called. I walked down the small hallway to the lab area in the back of the clinic, where Tobias was washing up.

"How's the oryx?" I asked.

"Doing okay so far," he said. "No sign of infection, which is good; I stitched her up pretty well. She may limp, but she'll be okay."

"Will the hunters pay to kill a limping oryx?" I asked.

He grimaced as he dried his hands. "I know. I take care of livestock I know is destined for dinner plates all the time, but there's something really off-putting about killing an animal just so you can show off its horns. I've never been a fan of canned hunts."

"Speaking of the game ranch, I don't know if you've heard, but they arrested Serafine today."

Tobias looked genuinely startled. "What?"

"We went to visit her down at the jail," I said. "I got her a good criminal attorney."

"With Rooster in charge, she'll need it. What I can't figure out is, what motive would they have? Other than the game ranch, that is. I wouldn't think that would be enough."

"I asked Aimee about what she was doing at the Whartons' ranch, but she wouldn't say a word about it. And there was some strange look between them... they know something they're not telling me."

"Well, if you were right about seeing Aimee's car, we can be pretty sure the two of them were seeing each other."

"Do you think there was more to it than that?"

"Well, if they were planning to get married and Mitch was in line to inherit the ranch, it certainly would be a motivation."

"Maybe," I said. "To be honest, I'm kind of surprised Rooster didn't arrest Peter."

"He's a hippie, but he's not a Wiccan," Tobias pointed out.

"Do you really think that's why he arrested her?"

"I'd like to think it wasn't a factor, but you know Rooster," he said. "On a more cheerful note, I have to go check on the oryx. Wanna come with me?"

"I'd love to."

"I named her Stella," he told me as he pushed open the door at the back of the clinic to the little barn area where he kept large animals.

"Stella?" I asked as we stepped outside. I followed him to the stall where Stella lay. She wasn't exactly perky, but she sure looked better than she had when we found her. Her flank was covered with bandages, and she didn't look to be in any hurry to get up.

"I've got her pretty sedated right now. As for the name, see the little star birthmark on her flank?"

"Awww... so cute!" I said. "She seems very sweet."

"She is," he said. "It kills me that I'm fixing her up so someone can shoot her. Sometimes I think I should have gone into practice in a city, where I dealt with pets."

"I'm glad you didn't," I said, wrapping my arms around him and leaning my head on his shoulder. "And I know you can't control what happens to them, but I'm glad you're here to take care of them."

He squeezed me back. "I'm just going to check her dressings, and then I'll be done. Then maybe we can go grab something to eat."

"Sounds like a plan," I said, "Except I need to get on the well thing."

"Well, maybe we can visit Lenny together," he said. "See if we can chivvy him along a bit."

"Thanks," I said. "I need all the help I can get. And then I'm going to see what I can find out about Bug Wharton."

A half hour later, we both turned up at Lenny's place, a dilapidated little bungalow a few blocks off the Town Square. Unfortunately, he wasn't there; we were greeted at the door by his wife.

"He went to Houston for the day," she said. "Sorry. " Before we could ask when he'd be back, her phone rang. "Gotta run… I'll tell him you stopped by. "

"Thanks," I said, but without high hopes. "Now what?" I asked Tobias as we walked back to the truck.

"Let's call Peter," Tobias suggested. "See if we can at least get your stock tanks filled."

I called, but there was no answer. I left a message; nobody was home today, it seemed. I slid my phone back into my pocket and turned to Tobias. "Now what?"

"Let's go get enchiladas," he suggested. "My treat, since you fed me dinner last night... and besides, the odds are you're going to be drilling a new well soon."

"I'll take you up on it," I said. We hopped into the truck for the short ride to Rosita's, and ten minutes later we were ensconced in a big booth with giant glasses of iced tea.

I had just placed my order—chicken chipotle enchiladas, which were hotter than heck and my absolute favorite—when Ed Zapp walked by the table and hailed my companion.

"Thanks for coming out to help with that steer last week," he said. "Sorry to call so late, but it looked like an emergency."

"You made the right call," Tobias said. "That's what I'm here for. Have you met Lucy?"

"We have," he said, and we shook hands. "We've met a couple of times, but we haven't had time to chat. You bought your grandmother's farm, right? The one belonged to the Vogels?"

"That's right," I confirmed.

"I hear you moved the old Ulrich house over there."

News traveled fast in Buttercup. "I did."

"Well, good luck with it," he said. "It's been haunted since I can remember."

"What kind of haunting?"

"Oh, the usual. Noises and such. And my wife, Ginny, swears she saw a lady in the upstairs window one time, but I ain't never seen nothin'. Still," he said, "some places kind of give me the heebie-jeebies, and that house is one of 'em. We went in once when we were kids on a lark, and whatever was in there put up such a racket we hightailed it out of there and never went back."

"Great," I said, feeling deflated.

"She's not had the best week," Tobias explained. "Her well went dry, she's discovered the house is supposed to be haunted, and now one of her friends was arrested."

"Over what happened to Bug Wharton? I heard," he said. "But I think Rooster ought to do a little more diggin'."

"Do you?" I asked.

"Where'd all his money come from? That's what I want to know. That property he bought was top dollar—and he paid in cash."

"Could it be family money?" I asked.

"I knew his family growing up," he said. "They were dirt poor. Could barely make it through winter some years."

"I heard he was in high tech," I said. "Maybe a start-up?"

"I heard somethin' about that, too, but here's the thing: Most of those folks crow all the time about how brilliant they are, about how much money they made when they sold. The Whartons don't say much of anything. Or didn't," he corrected himself.

"So, he never said who he worked for?" That should be easy enough to find out, I thought.

"Not a peep."

"Any idea if he had any feuds with anyone?" I asked.

"Well, the whole town saw what happened with that new witch lady. And that hippie farmer Peter Swenson was picketing his place just the other day with a bunch of crazy Austinites."

Not what I was hoping to hear. I was sure it was on Rooster's radar, too. "Anyone else?" I prodded.

"I did hear something the other day, now that you mention it," he told me. "Some Houston lady came to town, stayed a few days. I heard there was somethin' of a kerfuffle."

"About what?" Tobias asked.

"I don't know, but she called one of the deputies over to the ranch."

"Why?"

"Domestic incident," he said. "That's all I know."

Tobias and I exchanged looks. "And no idea who she was?" I asked.

He shook his head and pulled a tin of Skoal out of his back pocket. "Nope. Any road, I gotta head out. Nice seein' you, and good luck untangling the mess out at the Whartons' ranch. Oh—and you better make sure your livestock's locked up at night."

"Why?"

"Word on the street is, there's something nasty on the loose.

Chapter 10

"A MOUNTAIN LION?" TOBIAS ASKED.

"Chupacabra, more like. George Skalicky claims he saw it down by the creek the other day, but I don't buy it. I'd say there's a mountain lion hangin' round."

"Whatever it is, it got one of the oryxes at the Safari Exotic Game Ranch," Tobias said. "I was guessing mountain lion, too."

"Two people claim they saw some kind of ugly, wolf-like thing. Personally, I say it's one of those coyote-wolf mixes. Either that, or overactive imaginations."

"There have been coyotes through here, but I've not heard of any coywolves in the area," Tobias said. Some folks had talked about coyote/wolf hybrids moving into Texas; they were much bigger than coyotes and more dangerous, according to some reports. I hoped he was wrong; one mountain lion was bad enough, but a pack of coywolves would make me very nervous. "I'll keep an ear out, though, and let my clients know to keep a close eye on their animals."

Ed nodded. "Let me know what you find out. In the meantime, I've got to head back to the ranch. Good to see y'all." He shook hands with Tobias, tipped an imaginary hat to me, then took a pinch of snuff and tucked it into the pocket of his cheek as he headed toward the door.

As he left, our waitress returned with our order. My mouth watered as she set down a plate smothered in enchiladas with spicy red sauce, refried beans, and rice.

I thanked the waitress and picked up my fork, suddenly starving. "Did you hear anything about a visitor from Houston?" I asked as I cut into the first enchilada.

"No, but I'm curious about that domestic incident. That might be something to look in to."

"I know absolutely nothing about their personal lives," I said, glancing around at the other diners and dropping my voice.

"Something tells me there's more there than we know about."

"I'm going to ask Opal about the domestic incident," I decided. "I'm going to check online to see if I can figure out where their money came from, too. Maybe there's some professional connection, some kind of bad blood, we don't know about."

"Even if there were, that wouldn't necessarily explain what happened to Bug," Tobias said. "It's not like he was murdered in Topeka. If anyone came to visit from out of town, we'd know about it."

"The woman from Houston was here, and nobody knew about it. And if someone tampered with the EpiPen, they didn't need to be there when he died."

"But if you're right, someone put bees in the truck, which means they had to be in town."

"There were a few folks from outside of Buttercup at the Witches' Ball," I pointed out. "Besides, it's possible that someone parked, put the bees in the truck, and took off."

Tobias took a bite of his enchilada, looking thoughtful. "Did Serafine know he was allergic to bees?"

"I don't know who knew. I never heard anything about it; then again, I wasn't exactly close with the Whartons."

"Aimee seems to have been," Tobias said.

"She's not admitting to it, though."

"If it means keeping her sister out of jail, she might change her mind," he pointed out.

I sighed. "Maybe I'll have her over to dinner and see if I can find anything else out. Although after this plate of enchiladas, I may not be hungry again for a week."

He laughed. "They are pretty filling," he said.

"And I don't have to use water jugs to wash the plates," I said with a rueful smile.

"Next stop: fire department," Tobias said.

I raised my iced tea glass. "Sounds like a plan."

The fire department wasn't much; it was a basic brick building with a giant garage door. Grass was sprouting up through cracks in the pavement outside, and there were a couple of pumper trucks parked in the back corner. "I hear y'all are having well trouble," Ethan Schenk said when Tobias and I pulled up into the parking lot.

"It ran dry a few days ago," I said, "and I can't get anybody out to drill yet. Lenny Froehlich thinks I need a new well, but there's no dowser around, and evidently, that's a prerequisite."

"Peter mentioned you were having trouble. Is it drilled, or dug?"

"I think it's drilled," I told him.

"Well, we can't fill the well, but if you've got stock tanks, we could fill 'em up for you," he offered. "You won't be able to drink it, but you can keep your crops and livestock watered."

"That would be a lifesaver," I said, relieved. "How much would it be?"

"I'll talk to Peter and we'll work something out. It's not free, but it's not too expensive, either."

"That would be amazing," I said. "How soon do you think you can come out?"

"Would tomorrow be too late?" he asked.

"I can make it till tomorrow," I said. "Thank you so much. Is there anything I can do to help?"

"Just make sure we can get to the tank," he said. "Why don't you give me your number and I'll let you know when I've got an amount and a time?"

I reeled off my number and he added it to his phone. "I should know by tonight," he said.

"Thanks a million. And if you know of any dowsers in the area, I'd love to talk to them."

"I don't, offhand, but I'll ask around." He hesitated. "By the way, I hear Aimee asked for your help."

"She did," I said. "Why?"

He shrugged. "Well, I was one of the ones called out to the Safari Exotic Game Ranch the other night," he said. "First responder."

"During the domestic incident?" I asked.

He nodded. "I hope Rooster's looking in to that woman from Houston as a possible suspect. She was pretty hot. She went after him with a cattle prod."

"A cattle prod?" Tobias asked. "Like an electric one?"

He nodded. "She got him twice. And once... well, I won't tell you where."

Tobias and I winced.

"Did they arrest her?"

"Bug didn't press charges." He shrugged. "Probably

didn't want to testify that she'd zapped him in the family jewels."

"I guess I can understand that," Tobias said, still looking pained.

Who was she?" I asked.

"Her name was Evelyn," he said. "She wasn't very happy with Bug."

"Why?"

"I don't know," he said. "I got the feelin' they were dating, but she thought he was seein' someone else."

"Oh?"

"Well, she called him a 'two-timing son of a...'" Ethan trailed off, turning pink. "You know."

"I can imagine," I said. "So, her name was Evelyn."

"Yes," he said. "She drove a big white Lexus. I didn't catch her last name, but I'm sure Rooster knows it."

If he did, I thought, he certainly wasn't going to share it with me. Fortunately, he wasn't the only person in the sheriff's office.

"Sounds like a suspect for sure," Tobias said.

"Somehow, I doubt she's on Rooster's radar, though," I pointed out.

"We don't always get the best and brightest out in the country," Ethan agreed. "Anyhow, I thought I'd pass it on, for what it's worth. I hope you can clear Serafine's name."

"I didn't know you knew each other."

He colored. "We went out once or twice. She's so sweet and kind... I just don't believe she has it in her to kill anyone."

Frankly, I didn't either. I was pretty sure Rooster was taking the easy way out.

"I'll see what I can find out," I said. "Thanks again for your help with the water."

"Anytime," he said. "This drought is a killer. Fire risk has us all on edge. We've had three calls this week already."

"I've been a bit nervous, too," I said. "It doesn't take much." I lived in a wood house, and things were tinder-dry right now. I'd seen a house in Buttercup go up in flames before; it happened fast, and it was terrifying to think about.

"No, it doesn't. There's a burn ban on, but at least two of these Houston hobby farmers have decided to burn brush in the last few weeks."

I shuddered. "It could be Bastrop all over again." Bastrop was in the heart of Texas's famous Lost Pines; the town had been devastated a few years back by massive, drought-fueled fires. Although the trees were starting to come back, long stretches of US Hwy 71 still looked like a moonscape.

"We don't have the pines, but we've got plenty of cedars," Ethan said. "This used to be a fire-regulated system—the oaks are made to withstand ground fires, and the cedars would go up in smoke—but there's a lot of overgrowth now. An out-of-control fire would be a major disaster."

"Let's hope it doesn't happen, then," I said with a shiver.

"Just keep the bushes and trees cut back from the house," he said. "Make a clear zone if you can."

"I'd love to, but I can't bring myself to cut down my shade trees."

"Well, then, keep it all watered."

"I will, once I get a well that works."

"That's right," he said. "Well, we'll get your stock tanks filled up, at least. But you might want to get on the well. And if recent weather is any indicator, you might want to drill extra deep."

"No kidding," I said. Things seemed to be getting hotter and dryer the last few years. I loved Buttercup, but the weather made me nervous.

Tobias checked his watch. "I hate to run, but I've got to get back to work," he said.

I smiled at Ethan. "Thanks for your help. I hope to see you tomorrow!"

"Be careful of fire," he warned again. "And do what you can about Serafine."

"I will," I promised. "And let me know if you hear anything else."

Opal's Chevy wasn't parked outside the sheriff's office when I drove past, so I didn't bother going in. I hated to think of Serafine being locked up in there—I mean, how many Texas Monthly magazines can you read in a sitting?—and made a mental note to drop by with a few cozy mysteries the next day. Although I hoped she'd be out on bail—or, preferably, with all charges dropped—soon.

The sun was setting over the gentle, rolling hills when I pulled into my long driveway. As always, I felt a deep sense of home as I drove up to the little yellow farmhouse that had been part of my life since I could remember. And hoped it would continue to be.

I headed inside and said hi to Chuck, then pulled on a jacket—the temperature was dropping as the sun dipped toward the horizon—before heading out to check on everything and everyone. Gidget, Hot Lips, Priscilla and Carrot were nosing at the fence, hoping for treats, and Blossom and Peony were checking—

as usual—the perimeter. Blossom had acquired a taste for the geraniums on the Town Square, and was always looking for a way to escape. The geraniums of summer were long gone, having been replaced with bright yellow chrysanthemums and big pumpkins, but I couldn't tell her that.

I fed everyone a few treats—Chuck had visited the rosebush and promptly headed back inside where it was warm—and went to retrieve the bucket, then remembered I still had an old pump I'd picked up at a garage sale in Houston hidden somewhere in the barn. I detoured to the barn, digging through the boxes I'd stacked in an empty stall, until I found it. It wasn't strong, but I didn't want to spend the money on a bigger one if I didn't have to. After a bit of jury-rigging—I clipped the hose to the pump, dropped it into the stock tank, and ran a very long extension cord to the house—I managed to get a trickle of somewhat sludgy water and spent the next hour moving up and down the rows, trying not to smash the seedlings with the hose and hoping Ethan was as good as his word.

As I walked up and down the rows, parceling out water to my rather limp lettuce and broccoli seedlings, I thought about what Ethan had told me about Bug and his mystery woman from Houston. I was sure Rooster knew about her. So why slap Serafine in jail so fast? Sure, they'd had an argument over the mead cauldron, but wouldn't zapping someone with an electric cattle prod indicate more of a motive? I hoped Opal could give me a lead to follow up on. If nothing else, I was guessing the mysterious Evelyn could tell me more about Bug than anyone in Buttercup. Except possibly Aimee, who was being rather cagey about things, considering her sister was in jail for murder.

So far, we had at least one viable suspect: Evelyn from Houston. And, potentially, Bug's brother Mitch, although I knew next to nothing about their relationship, much less what he might have stood to gain from killing his brother. And Aimee was mixed in there somehow, too. I thought back to our visit to the ranch; it had definitely been her car, and her voice had been familiar. I didn't think I'd been mistaken. But what about? I'm sure if the two were an item, he'd know at least something about it, but I doubted he'd want to talk to me. He didn't seem to want us around; I had the feeling he was hiding something.

I looked over at the old homestead, thinking of all the secrets people keep—and wondered what secrets the little house might be keeping. What had that noise been the other night, anyway? I finished watering the row and walked back to the stock tank, carefully dragging the hose so as not to crush any baby plants. There was only six inches of water left in the tank; if Ethan didn't come tomorrow, my goose— or at least my broccoli—was cooked.

I coiled the hose next to the tank and walked back down to the little house, feeling a little frisson of unease as I got closer. What had that noise been last night?

The house was quite small: two rooms flanking a hallway that led from front to back in the downstairs, with a loft that stretched the length of the house upstairs. If I ever found the money to pay for it, I was hoping to use it as a rental.

It was going to take some work, though; and if the place was haunted, I wasn't sure how many return guests I'd get.

I walked around the house first, studying it yet again for signs of a loose board or shutter, but there was nothing I could see. The wind had died down; the air was still, and the only sounds were the distant bleating of the goats and the haunting call of a whippoorwill from the direction of the dry creek. As I rounded the front of the house, I paused, listening, then took a step onto the front porch.

The wood bowed and creaked beneath me, and I quickly moved to a slightly sounder-looking board, then tiptoed to the front door, praying the whole house wouldn't cave in around me. If it survived the weight of both Tobias and Peter, I told myself, I should be okay.

The door opened with a creak, and after a moment's hesitation, I stepped into the dusty interior.

The inside of the house was dim, the light of the setting sun feeble as it passed through the dirty windows. The wood boards in the hallway were worn, and for a moment I had the fleeting sensation that I could feel all the lives that had passed through the little house. Whose hand had painted the delicate blue stencils at the tops of the walls? Was it the vanished girl's mother, trying to make her house a home? Had she also sewed curtains for the windows? Was one of the rooms a kitchen? There was no fireplace; had she followed the tradition of having a separate kitchen outside, to keep the heat out in the summer and cut the risk of fire?

I shivered again at the thought of fire. At least the wind had died down; that was a help. I took a step into the room to the left, reaching up to touch the bottom of one of the stenciled patterns; I could see the brush strokes. How long ago had she painted it? I wondered. I knew it was a she. What were her dreams? I thought about my own life. I'd considered having children, but my ex wasn't exactly the paternal type, and things with

Tobias were still... forming. We'd never thought about children. What would it be like to have children waking up in the upstairs of my grandmother's house?

Too soon to think about that, I told myself, swatting the thought away and taking a step back toward the hallway, expecting the banging to start at any minute. It didn't; if there was a ghost, he or she must be napping. I hoped that would continue.

I took a few deep breaths and then inspected the narrow, rickety staircase to the second floor. Without thinking about it too much, I grabbed the banister and gingerly stepped onto the first tread. It bowed, but didn't break, and I made it up four more—high enough to peek into the loft area.

Whatever had been in the loft had been taken out before the house was moved; the area was empty. There was no sign of anything that could have made the noise I'd heard. I waited for another few minutes, both hoping for and dreading a recurrence, but there was nothing but the sound of the goats in the distance; the whippoorwill seemed to have moved on.

I was about to give up and head back down the steps when something caught my eye. On the top step, something gleamed in the fading light. I reached for it, but it was too far.

Saying a little prayer to my beleaguered guardian angel—if she hadn't long ago quit in despair—I took another two tentative steps up the narrow staircase, praying the treads wouldn't collapse under me. I stifled a sneeze at the dust I was inhaling as I reached for the source of the gleam.

It was a gold chain. I tugged at it, but it didn't come. It appeared to be caught between the boards of the steps. I took another step, saying another little prayer, and examined the top step. The riser appeared to have come loose from the tread. I curled my fingers around the edge of it and gave a gentle tug. It moved about an inch. I pulled a little harder, and the old wood released, exposing a small cavity.

The gold chain was the end of a necklace that had been tucked in behind the step. I loosened the chain from where it was caught, and tugged gently. A dusty cameo slid into the dim light. I picked it up, brushing the grime from the ivory-colored face. Whose had it been... and why was it hidden behind the riser? Cradling the cameo in my hand, I peered into the dark cavity, wondering if anything else was hidden. I was in luck; there was a small leather-bound book. I gently removed it from its hiding place and opened it, but the words were written in a flowery, hard-to-read script in a language I didn't understand—German, from the looks of it. I leafed through the old book, which was only half-full—a diary?—and looked to see if there was anything else in the cavity.

There was. It was a rusty knife, and it looked like it was caked with dried blood.

Chapter 11

"HELLO?" I CALLED. I'M NOT sure why. Maybe I figured if this was what the ghost wanted me to find, it might answer.

It didn't, but I still didn't feel like hanging around.

I gathered what I'd found—except for the knife, which I decided I didn't want to take with me—and hurried down the stairs, praying the treads would hold but too anxious to be out of the house to go any slower. I burst through the front door and took a deep breath of the clean, dust-free air, shaking myself as if that would dispel the eerie feeling. It didn't work.

Once I'd caught my breath, I walked around the outside of the house again, looking for a loose board, a flapping piece of metal roof—anything that could have explained the noises we'd heard the other night. There was nothing, though, and no wind today, anyway. With the diary and the cameo in my hands, I turned toward the house, still feeling spooked.

I had just made myself a cup of tea to steady my nerves when I heard the sound of tires on the dirt driveway. I looked through the window; it was my friend Molly. She'd been in Dallas for her sister's fiftieth birthday party; she must have just gotten back.

"I leave for a week, and everything goes to heck!" my friend said as she got out of her truck and headed to the front porch. She wore a blue sweater and faded boot-cut jeans. Her graying hair was pulled back into a ponytail, and her brown eyes crinkled into a smile when she saw me.

"I'm so glad you're home," I said. "How was your trip?"

"It was good," she said. "But I'm happy to be back. I think I'm allergic to Dallas."

"I'm not a big fan of it, either," I replied, giving her a hug. "I was just having a cup of tea; come join me."

"I'd love to! It's much quieter here than at home; I missed everyone, but they can be pretty chaotic."

"I can't believe they let you get away," I told her. Molly lived on an active farm with four kids, her husband, a dog, and lots of livestock.

"The house is a mess; I walked in, then told them I was coming to visit you and they had two hours to get it squared away."

I laughed. "What are the odds they'll do it?"

"It won't be perfect, but there are so many dirty dishes they've started eating cereal out of coffee mugs. I told them they at least had to get the kitchen cleared up and the clothes off the living-room floor."

"Maybe I'm glad I don't have kids after all," I said.

"It makes it a lot easier to keep the house straight," she agreed, glancing around at my relatively tidy kitchen. "But fill me in on the news. I hear Bug got bitten by a bug."

"He did," I said as I poured her a cup of tea and sat down across from her at my big pine table. "And Serafine's in the town jail."

"I heard that, too," she said. "I can't imagine Serafine hurting anyone... she's one of the most empathetic people I know."

"She was pretty angry at Bug," I said. "And she's very protective of animals."

"That's true," Molly conceded. "Do you think she did it?"

"I don't, actually. I think Rooster's just being lazy."

"What I don't understand is, if he died of a bee sting, how could it be murder?"

"I think someone messed with his EpiPen," I told her. "And snuck bees into his truck to make sure he got stung."

"Do you think it might have been Serafine? She's got beehives, after all."

"She did have a big showdown with Bug at the Witches' Ball... and she burned his cup after he was done with it. I told him about the cone of paper with the dead bee in it—it was in the front seat of his truck—but Rooster ignored me. I think his theory is that she put bee venom in the cup and somehow managed to sabotage his EpiPen, too."

"So, you're thinking someone else did it, and then put the bees in the truck to make sure he had to use it?"

"It's a theory." I took a sip of tea and put my cup down. "I just realized the twist of paper almost had to be put in the truck after Bug parked and got out. Mitch was in the passenger seat; if the paper was there before, he would have crushed it by sitting on it."

"So someone at the Witches' Ball put the bees in the truck. It could have been anyone; there are hives on the property."

"There are," I said. "If we can get Rooster to listen to us, it might clear Serafine. If she was at the cauldron the whole time, that is; we had a card reading done, so I wasn't watching."

"But lots of people were. There were tons of witnesses." She took a sip of her tea. "Someone might have seen someone near his truck in the parking lot, too. It's hard to do anything in Buttercup without someone noticing."

"It's worth asking around," I said, feeling more hopeful. "Also, Ethan Schenk down at the fire station told me a woman from Houston hit Bug in the family jewels with an electric cattle prod a day or two before he died. Ethan was one of the first responders; Rooster knew about it, too."

She cringed. "Ouch!"

"Totally," I agreed. "If you're willing to go after someone with a cattle prod, you've clearly got a beef with them."

"Do you know who it is?"

"I have a first name. I'm hoping Opal can tell me the rest; she wasn't at the sheriff's office when I drove by this evening."

"Poor Serafine," Molly said.

"I know. I may swing by with a few paperbacks for her tomorrow. I got her hooked up with an attorney; hopefully, she'll be out soon on bail."

"Hopefully." She sighed. "For a small town, there seems to be a whole lot going on."

"I know. My well ran dry this week, I can't find a dowser, and that old house I got talked into moving here seems to be haunted."

"Haunted?"

I told her about the weird banging noises, and then showed her the diary and the cameo I'd found hidden behind the riser. "There was a rusty knife, too, but I left it behind."

"Gross," she said.

"Even though it's probably been there for a hundred years or more, it looks like there's blood on it."

She wrinkled her nose and picked up the small book. "No wonder the place is haunted, if there's a bloody knife hidden in it. I heard they found someone murdered on the front porch back in the eighteen hundreds... maybe you found the murder weapon."

"That's a cheerful thought."

She leafed through the small, leather-bound book. "Looks like a diary. What language is this in?"

"I think it's German."

"I think so, too," she said. "But the script is really hard to read. There's a date here, though..." She pointed to the top of the page.

"Looks like 1839," I said. "That's pretty close to the time of Ilse's disappearance. Is there a name in it?"

"No," she said, turning to the first page. "At least not in the front."

"I'll bet Maria can read it. I'll have to take it to her to see what she thinks. But I'm having serious second thoughts about moving the house to the farm."

"I'm sure it will be fine once you get it renovated."

"If," I said. "I told you, my well ran dry this week; I've got to pay for that first."

She looked over at the counter, where I had four jugs of drinking water. "Oh, no, Lucy... I'm so sorry. I wondered why you had water jugs... What are you going to do?"

I told her about Lenny's visit. "The dowser died, and I think Lenny's been dodging me ever since. I'm hoping Ethan down at the fire department will refill my stock tanks today, but I've got to come up with a longer-term solution. Do you know any dowsers?"

"Not offhand, but I'll ask around," she told me. As

she took another sip of her tea, which she'd barely touched, her phone buzzed. She rolled her eyes as she glanced at it. "Apparently, they're ready for me to come home," she announced, turning the phone so that I could see it. "They even texted me a picture of the kitchen."

"Not too bad," I said. "I'll bet they didn't wipe the counters down, though."

"I know," she said. "What's up with that? Anyway," she said, standing up, "I guess I should head back. Why don't you come over for dinner sometime this week?"

"I'd love to," I said, giving her a hug. "I'm glad you're back."

"Me too," she said. "Sounds like it's been a rough couple of days here."

"Maybe things will turn around now that you're back."

"Here's hoping," she said, giving me a hug. "Let me know what you find out about that diary," she said.

"I've got to find someone who speaks German. But first, I've got a few other things to take care of."

"Never a dull moment, is there?"

"If only," I said with a rueful smile.

Molly had only been gone a few minutes when I heard a truck coming up the driveway. I glanced out the window; it was the pumper truck, with Ethan in the driver's seat.

"The reinforcements have arrived," I informed Chuck, who looked up at me and cocked his head to one side. I threw on a sweatshirt and headed out to meet Ethan. "Thanks so much for coming out!" I called as I stepped off the front porch. He'd stopped the truck and was surveying the stock tank closest to the driveway. The goats were eyeing him with interest, probably hoping he had snacks in his pockets.

"Is this the one you want filled?" he asked.

"Both would be better, but if you can only do this one, that would be great," I said. "Need any help?"

"Let's get the hose over to the tank. I'll start it going, and you let me know when it's full."

"Thanks," I said. Together, we put the hose end into the tank, and I watched as he headed back to the truck and started the pump. It didn't take long for the tank to fill. Unfortunately, I knew it also wouldn't take long for the tank to empty.

"Any rain in the forecast yet?" I asked once he'd turned off the water and we were putting the hose back onto the truck.

"Not that I've seen," he said. "There are supposed to be high winds in a couple of days, though. We're all a little nervous about that." He turned to look at my little house. "You should probably cut back some of those trees," he advised me a second time.

"I know," I said. "But the shade is awfully nice in the summer."

He shook his head, then turned to the subject I suspected was on his mind. "Find out anything else about what happened to Bug?"

"I'm working on it," I said.

"I stopped by to see Serafine earlier, but Rooster wouldn't let me in. I'm worried about her," he said.

"I am, too," I said. "I asked around about where the Whartons got their fortune the other day; someone told me he'd worked for a company called TechGenerator up in Illinois for a while."

"What kind of business were they in?"

"Some kind of government contract work, I think. I'll look it up."

"I heard something else, too," he said. "Guess who inherits the ranch?"

"Mitch Wharton?"

He nodded.

"Does Rooster know about that?"

"I don't know."

"You might want to mention it to him," I suggested. "He won't want to hear it from me."

"One more thing... Quinn's ex just got a job at the ranch."

"Jed Stadtler?"

He nodded. "Helping feed and take care of the animals. Said he wanted to be back in town."

"Why can't he just stay away?" I asked.

"He's bad news, I know," Ethan said. "He was down at the station the other day complaining about Quinn."

"What did he say?"

"That she made it all up, got him thrown into jail for nothing."

"I was there when he attacked her," I said. "If he'd had a gun on him, neither of us might still be here."

"Bad news," he said. "Is she still having trouble with him?"

"He's been trouble since the day they met," I told him, feeling a sense of foreboding.

"I'll keep an eye out," he said. "Tell her if she needs to learn to use a gun, I can help."

"I'll pass it on," I said. I knew she was against having a gun, but with Jed in town, she might change her mind. "What do I owe you for the water, by the way?"

He waved it away. "It's nothing," he said.

"Are you sure?"

"Happy to be of assistance," he said, and swung himself back into the truck. "Thanks for helping Serafine. I feel better knowing you're on it."

"I'll do what I can," I said. I just hoped it would be enough.

Chapter 12

I HAD JUST FINISHED CUTTING UP pumpkins and sterilizing a batch of Mason jars for pumpkin butter when there was a knock at the door. It was Maria Ulrich.

"I hope you don't mind my coming by," she said, "but Molly told me you found something at the house."

"I did," I told her. "Sit down and I'll grab them for you. Can I get you some tea? I was just making pumpkin butter."

"I'd love to, but I can't stay long. I just wanted to see what you found—and where you found it."

I rinsed my hands and retrieved the diary and the cameo brooch from the hutch in the living room, handing them to Maria, who received them as if they were holy artifacts.

"This is amazing," she breathed. "It was in the house the whole time, and I didn't know! Molly said you found these under the stairs?"

"The top riser had a hidden compartment behind it," I told her. I hesitated before adding, "There was a knife in there, too, but I left it." I didn't mention the blood.

She leafed through the onionskin pages. "It's German, all right. The handwriting is flowery, but I can read some of the words."

"What does it say?"

"It's hard to decipher without a dictionary... but can I take it with me?"

"Of course," I said.

"And this pin," she said, touching it reverently. "I wonder which one of my ancestors this belonged to?"

"Maybe the diary will tell you," I said.

"And maybe the secret of what happened to Ilse Ulrich will finally be solved," she said.

If Comanches had abducted Ilse, I thought it highly unlikely they'd paused to give her time to record the event in her diary, but I just smiled.

She looked up and sniffed the air. "What smells so good?"

"Pumpkin butter," I told her. "I sell it at the markets on weekends."

"Oooh, that sounds terrific. I'll have to pick some up at the market this week," she said.

"Or you can take a jar with you now. I sterilize it, but it has to be refrigerated, just in case," I warned her.

"It won't last that long anyway," she said, taking another appreciative sniff and then hugging the diary to her chest. "Do you mind if I take a look in the house to see where it came from? Maybe there's something else hidden there."

"Of course. I'd go with you, but I'm kind of in the middle of things here," I told her. "The riser is at the top of the stairs."

"Thanks. I'll be back!" she said.

As Maria stepped outside, the phone rang. I rinsed my hands quickly and picked it up, smiling when Tobias said hello. "How are things at Dewberry?" he asked.

"Better," I told him. "I just got water!"

"Terrific! No word from Lenny, I presume?"

"Of course not, but Ethan filled up the stock tank for free. And I found out the name of the company Bug was working for; Ethan is pretty anxious to get Serafine off the hook."

"He's sweet on her, isn't he?"

"He sure is. And Maria Ulrich is down nosing around the house." I told him what I'd found. "She's going to translate the diary; maybe it'll shed some light on who's causing all that banging."

"I think that banging has a more scientific explanation," Tobias told me.

"Well, when you show me what's causing it, I'll be happy to go with it. How's the oryx?" I asked.

"Better today," he said, "but I'm heading out to the Safari Exotic Game Ranch to check out some new livestock, and I thought you might want to go with me."

"Absolutely I would," I said.

"I've got a few things to take care of, but I'll be over in a little bit."

"I just have to finish up this pumpkin butter and I'll be ready to go."

I had cut up several pumpkins; now, I weighed them before putting them into a big stainless-steel pot I'd picked up at the antique fair, then stirred in brown sugar, cardamom, allspice, and cloves. Before long, the mixture in the pot began to simmer, making the kitchen smell deliciously of pumpkin pie. As the pumpkin cooked down, I pulled Google up on my computer and typed in TechGenerator.

Whatever it had been, TechGenerator was no longer in operation; there were a few business listings, and it was described as a software company, but there was no indication of what kind of software the company wrote, and the website was defunct. I searched "IPO TechGenerator," but came up empty. Either the name had changed with no fanfare, or the Whartons hadn't gotten rich off selling a start-up.

I gave the pumpkin a stir, adjusted the heat, and then ran a search on Bug Wharton. His real name, as it turned out, was Jerome; although I wasn't a big fan of the name Bug, I could see that some might think it was better than the alternative. I got a listing for him living in Ohio; I wrote down the address and looked it up on Zillow, expecting a mansion, but it appeared to be a modest house in a modest neighborhood. I checked on the pumpkin—it was cooking down nicely—and saw he'd lived in Ohio for fifteen years; before that, there was an address in Houston and one in Smithville. Was Evelyn an old flame from his Houston days?

After petering out on Bug, I looked up his brother, Mitch. To my surprise, four news articles popped up at the top of the screen, and I immediately knew where the money had come from.

The pumpkin butter was just about done by the time I'd exhausted my research capabilities, and I processed each batch in the blender, then transferred the spicy, deep orange butter to the sterilized jars and put them in the refrigerator. As I licked the spoon, savoring the rich fall flavor, I heard Tobias pull up outside.

Chuck trotted to the door to greet him, barking excitedly as the veterinarian headed up the walk. "Come on in!" I called when he got to the door.

"You ready?"

"I am," I told him as he joined me in the kitchen and kissed me on top of the head. "I found out how the Whartons made their money."

"How?"

"Mitch won the lottery in Florida," I said.

Tobias looked at the screen and let out a low whistle. "Five million dollars? That'll buy you a lot of oryxes."

"It sure will," I said.

"But I thought Bug was the one with the money," Tobias said. "Mitch always seemed like a sidekick."

"I got that impression, too," I said. "No wonder they were able to afford the ranch, though."

"If Mitch was the winner, that kind of takes him out of the equation as a suspect, don't you think?" Tobias commented. "If anything, it'd be more likely for Bug to want to kill Mitch."

"Who bought the property?" I asked. I pulled up the website for the ranch, wincing at the photo of a dead springbok surrounded by a smiling family, then typed the address of the appraisal district website for Fayette County.

"Jerome Wharton," I said. "It's the only name on the deed."

"I'd ask if they had wealthy parents, but word around town is that they grew up dirt poor."

"Maybe Jerome did make money from his company," I speculated, "and Mitch spent all his lottery winnings and became dependent on his brother."

"Did you find anything out about his company?"

"Not much," I answered, showing him the websites I'd pulled up. "Nothing but a few addresses and a Better Business Bureau listing in Ohio. The last listing was from about two years ago."

"When did Mitch win the lottery?"

I flipped to the other tab. "Eighteen months ago," I said.

"Unless he's the one who funded the ranch for Bug,

he went through that money awfully fast. Even with a big tax bite, that's a lot of cash to go through in a year and a half."

"Unless he bought the ranch for his brother?"

"Why would he do that?" Tobias asked. "Besides, I got the clear impression that Bug ran the show."

"Bug was the older brother, wasn't he? Maybe it's just family dynamics," I theorized. "Maybe Mitch was somehow being controlled by his brother, got tired of it, and did him in."

Tobias put his hands on my shoulders. "I wish we knew what was in his will. Maybe Mindy could help find out. If the estate is being probated, it might be public record."

I bristled a bit at the mention of Mindy Flynn, his ex. I knew she was remarrying, but she was gorgeous, and I still felt a jolt of jealousy when her name came up. "It might help."

"There's something we're missing here," Tobias said. "Let me think on it. But in the meantime, let's head over to the ranch.

"Let me check in with Maria, and we'll go," I said, doing a last wipe of the counters and putting a jar of the still-hot pumpkin butter into a sturdy paper bag before following Tobias outside. "She's been down there for forever; I hope she's okay."

There was no sign of Maria when we went outside; she must still be in the little house. "Well, at least the house is still standing," I said. "I wonder if she's pulling up floorboards?"

"Just as long as she puts them back," Tobias said.

We had just gotten to the front porch when the door opened and Maria stepped out.

"Find anything?" I asked.

She shook her head. "I searched the whole place," she said. "I didn't find anything other than the knife you told me about," she said. "No weird noises, either; I think that whole haunting thing was just a story."

"We heard some banging the other day, but Tobias here is convinced it's a loose board or something."

Maria gingerly stepped off the porch, then turned to look at the house. "These walls have seen so many things; I wish they could talk."

"At least you have a diary now," I pointed out. "Maybe that will solve some family mysteries."

She looked down at the book in her hand. "It's going to take some work to read, but I'm excited about it. Maybe I could publish it as part of the German Heritage thing? Think Texas A&M Press would be interested?"

"It's worth looking in to," I told her. "And maybe you'll find out what that cameo and that knife were doing in there, too."

"I'll let you know," she said. "Thanks again for saving the house; I'm bringing it up at the meeting tomorrow and asking if we can help you with the preservation."

"Thanks," I said. "I brought you a jar of pumpkin butter, by the way," I told her, proffering the bag. "It's still very hot, though; be careful!"

Her eyes lit up. "Ooh, thank you. That'll be great on my toast in the morning."

"It will be," I confirmed. "We're headed out now, but let me know what you find out about the diary."

"Will do," she said. "And keep your fingers crossed about that meeting!"

I would. Any help I could get financially right now was more than welcome.

There were more vehicles than usual parked at the Safari Exotic Game Ranch when we arrived. Tobias passed by the main compound, which was fairly stuffed with luxury SUVs, and headed to the barn. "I wonder if Jed's here?" I mused as Tobias pulled up next to Bug's giant extended-cab truck.

"I wish he'd just leave town and never come back," Tobias replied.

"So does Quinn."

Despite the number of SUVs we'd seen parked near the entrance, there was no sign of anyone in the area of the barn. "If folks are out hunting, do you think it's safe?" I asked.

"As long as we don't go off into the woods, we should be okay," he said. As he spoke, there was a gunshot in the distance; I jumped, wincing.

"Those poor animals."

He grimaced. "I know."

Together, we headed into the barn. The ibexes that had been there the other day were no longer penned; I found myself wondering if one of them had just been shot. In their place were four kangaroos.

"Kangaroos?" I asked. "Really?"

He sighed. "Kind of sick, I know. At least it's a change of pace for me." He looked around. "I wonder where José is?"

"I'm more worried about Jed," I said in a low voice.

As if I'd conjured him, Quinn's ex walked into the barn, a bucket swinging from his right hand. Jail hadn't diminished him, unfortunately; if anything, he was more muscular than when he'd been convicted. He was over six feet tall and built like a brick. He stopped short when he saw me. "What are you doing here?" His voice was menacing.

Tobias stepped between us. "We're here to look at the kangaroos," he told Jed in a firm voice. "Is José here?"

"I haven't seen him," Jed said, surly. He jabbed a finger at me. "Why is she here?"

"She's helping me," Tobias informed him. "If you haven't seen José, we'll go look in the office."

Jed said nothing, but watched as Tobias and I left the barn and headed for the trailer José used as an office.

"He gives me the creeps," I murmured.

"He should," Tobias told me as he mounted the two steps to the trailer door. "He's trouble." He was about to knock when he noticed the door was ajar. "José?" he called.

There was a groaning sound from inside the trailer. Tobias looked back at me.

"That doesn't sound good," I said.

He pushed the door open, and I followed him in to the small, dark space. There was another groan from the corner, where José lay crumpled on the floor.

Chapter 13

TOBIAS RUSHED OVER TO HIM. "What happened?"

"Coffee... sick..." he moaned. I looked up at the cluttered desk; there was a half-drunk cup of coffee.

"Call 911," Tobias told me. I reached for the phone and dialed.

As I relayed our location and the information to the dispatcher, Tobias checked José's vitals and then sniffed the coffee. "It's bitter," he said. "I don't know what it is, but I'm guessing he might have been poisoned." He grabbed his bag and pulled out a bottle and a dosing cup.

"Can you drink this?" he asked José.

José, looking pale, nodded. Tobias filled the cup with a steady hand and turned to me. "Help me prop him up?"

"Of course," I said, and helped him sit up as Tobias guided the cup to his mouth. He gagged, but it went down. Tobias grabbed the metal wastepaper basket from next to the desk just in time. After he'd emptied his stomach, Tobias pulled a jar of charcoal capsules from his bag and glanced around the little office, his eyes fixing on the water dispenser in the corner. He hurried over and filled a cup, then offered José several black capsules.

"Take these," Tobias ordered.

"But..."

"Just try," he said. "It'll help neutralize whatever was in the coffee." José obeyed, managing to stomach what Tobias gave him, and sagged back against me.

"Am I gonna die?" he croaked.

"We're doing everything we can for you," Tobias said. "How long ago did you drink the coffee?"

"Ten minutes, I think." José made a gagging noise.

"Just relax," Tobias said. "See if you can keep it down; it should absorb the poison, if that's what it is. Any other symptoms?"

"Stomach cramp," he said, doubling over. "Bad."

"Easy, José," Tobias said in the strong, calm voice I had heard him use with animals. "The paramedics are on their way."

"Where did you get the coffee?" I asked.

"From the pot over there," he said. There was about an inch of murky liquid left in the glass coffeepot. I sniffed the cup, which had been doctored with creamer; there was a bitter, acrid scent that didn't smell like coffee. Then I grabbed a Kleenex from the box on the desk and used it to ease the coffeepot out from the machine without disturbing any fingerprints, taking a whiff of the contents. No bitterness.

"Is this the creamer you used?" I asked, pointing to the canister of Coffee-Mate next to the pot.

He nodded.

"Does anyone else use creamer?"

"Yes," he said. "But not Splenda." He pointed to the yellow bag on the shelf above the coffeemaker.

"Do you have any latex gloves?"

Tobias handed me a pair from his bag; I put them on, then took the bag down and gave it a sniff.

"It smells bitter, but I'm not sure if that's normal," I said.

"Let me take a whiff," Tobias said. I offered him the bag, and he sniffed at it. "I don't know either," he confessed. "We'll make sure it gets checked out, though. We should send a sample to the hospital; I'll fill a syringe with some of the coffee, too, just so they have something to analyze."

I set the bag of Splenda on the cluttered desk and glanced around the trailer. It was a mess; there were piles of paper everywhere, with shipping notices from Africa and invoices from feed company. I accidentally brushed a pile of credit-card statements on a beaten-up credenza. As I picked them up, I noticed some very large charges from a resort called Coushatta, in Louisiana. It must have been a luxury resort; there were at least two charges in excess of ten thousand dollars. As I gathered the rest of the statements, I heard footsteps on the stairs to the trailer. A moment later, the door opened and Mitch Wharton burst in. "José..." he began, then trailed off when he saw me standing by the credenza with a pile of papers in my hand. "What are you doing here?" he asked, and his eyes flicked to the yellow bag, which I'd set down on the desk. "Where's José?"

"Over there," I told him, pointing to the other end of the trailer, where Tobias was still ministering to the man.

"What happened?" Mitch asked. "Forget his insulin?"

"He's diabetic?" Tobias asked.

Mitch nodded.

"I don't think that's what caused this," Tobias said.

"It's got to be," Mitch insisted. "Some kind of diabetic

coma or something. Maybe his insulin was messed up."

Before Tobias could answer, there was the sound of sirens; the paramedics had arrived.

"He's stable," the EMT announced as they moved José to a gurney and wheeled him into the back of the ambulance twenty minutes later.

"It was his diabetes, right?" Mitch asked.

"It doesn't look like it," she said, "but I suppose it could be related. We'll know more when we get to the hospital."

Mitch looked unconcerned. "This is probably a big deal about nothing."

"Is he going to be okay?" I asked.

"We'll see," she said. "If it was something he ate, you made a good call with the ipecac and the charcoal," she told Tobias. "It might have made all the difference."

"Are the police coming?" I asked.

She nodded. "They should be on their way."

"We'll stay until they get here," Tobias told her.

Mitch waved Tobias away. "I'll wait till they get here. No need for you to waste your time."

"They may have some questions for us," Tobias countered. "Lucy and I really should be here."

Mitch paused for a moment, looking like he was deciding on a course of action, before changing tacks. "Did you get a chance to check out the new arrivals?" he asked, changing the subject.

"I took a brief look at them, but I was hoping to see the paperwork; that's why we came to the trailer," Tobias said.

"I can find it for you," Mitch suggested, starting

toward the desk.

Tobias held up a hand. "It's okay. Why don't you show me the kangaroos? We can all go together, and we'll come back here when the police arrive. We can get the paperwork later; I can do a quick examination in the meantime."

Mitch hesitated, then nodded. "All right, then. We'll go check them out."

Tobias and I followed the rancher out of the trailer. "It looks like you've got quite a crowd here this weekend," I said, trying to shift the subject. "Business must be pretty good."

"It's not bad.," Mitch shrugged. "We're trying to bring in some more interesting game to try to drum up more business; we've got a few giraffes on order."

"Giraffes?" I asked. Why on God's green earth would anyone want to shoot a giraffe? Then again, I thought, looking at the cute kangaroos huddled in the corner of the pen, why would anyone want to shoot a kangaroo?

I stood outside the pen as Tobias let himself in, using a soothing tone as he approached the poor creatures. As he squatted down to take a closer look at them, the ambulance pulled away from the barn. I waved to the paramedic and said a brief prayer that José would be okay. In fact, when the police arrived, I planned to suggest that they post a guard on him at the hospital; if someone had tried to kill José to keep him from sharing something he knew, they might try again. If it was Rooster, he would probably ignore me, but at least I felt I should mention it.

Mitch, who hadn't joined Tobias in the pen, kept glancing back at the trailer as Tobias worked. "I really should go get that paperwork," he suggested.

"It can wait," Tobias repeated as he checked the ears

of the smallest kangaroo. When he released it, it shook itself and hopped away. "Besides, from what I can see, everyone looks pretty healthy."

"Good, good," Mitch said.

"At least that's some good news, eh?" I said. "It's been a rough week. First Bug, and now José."

"Yeah," he said absently.

Before he could say anything else, Jed jogged up to the scene. "What's going on?" he asked. "I saw an ambulance tear out of here.

"José had some kind of diabetic reaction or something," Mitch said, squinting at Jed. "I hope you're up for some overtime."

"Why?"

"They just took him to the hospital. I need someone to help take care of the animals while he's out."

I couldn't think of anyone less qualified to take care of animals—Jed had once kicked poor Chuck against a wall because he was angry—but I swallowed back my objection.

"I'm on it," Jed said. "Just give me a list." As he spoke, a police car rolled up. Jed eyed it nervously. "I'll get to work and check in later," he said before melting into the undergrowth not far from the barn.

Rooster stepped out of his Crown Victoria, his eyes narrowing when he saw me. "You again," he said, his red wattle jiggling. "You always turn up where there's trouble. What's this all about anyway?"

"We found one of the Whartons' workers—José— on the floor of the trailer. It looked like he might have been poisoned, so I gave him ipecac and charcoal. I took a small sample of the coffee with a syringe and sent it with the paramedics, along with a little bit of the artificial sweetener he used, but we left the coffee cup there on the desk."

"Why'd you do that?"

"It has a strange, bitter smell; if he ingested something, the hospital may be able to figure out what it is from the sample. Lucy and I aren't sure, but we think there might be something in the Splenda." Tobias gestured toward the yellow bag next to the coffeepot.

"Did y'all touch that stuff, contaminate it with fingerprints?"

"We put gloves on before touching anything," Tobias replied. "Except for José, of course, and the doorknob."

Rooster squinted at the coffee cup. "Sure it wasn't just a heart attack or something?"

"It didn't look like a heart attack," Tobias said. "I'm not an MD, but I'd say it was something he ingested. I told the paramedic they should take a look at the samples at the hospital and do some blood testing, too, in case it was something else."

"So y'all just walked in and found him on the floor?"

"That's right," Tobias said.

"Seems you have a habit of findin' almost-dead bodies, Miz Resnick. And dead ones, too."

"It's a small town," Tobias said. "And I was there for both of them, too."

"I'll check with the hospital," Rooster said. "If they find anything, I'll call out the detectives. In the meantime, I'm going to lock this place up."

"But if someone else has the key," I pointed out, "they'd be able to get in and get rid of any evidence."

He gave me a sour look. It was obvious that hadn't occurred to him.

"Do you have a chain and padlock or something?" Tobias suggested. "That would keep people out."

"I've probably got something in the trunk," Rooster

said. Together, we followed him out of the trailer. He dug around in the cluttered trunk of his car for a while, then came up with two short two-by-fours and some nails. "This'll have to do. No hammer, but I can use some of the wood to pound the nails in."

"I'll hammer it if you'll hold it," Tobias offered. Together, they used two-by-fours to nail the door shut while I watched; as Rooster held up the board, Tobias hammered in the nails. "There'll be some damage, but they can always patch the holes when it comes off."

"I hope they don't need anything in there," I said. "How long do you think it'll be before you know anything?"

"It's police business," he informed me.

"Of course," I said, trying not to sound too irritated.

Rooster gave me a slow, unpleasant smile. "Your friend had better hope it's not poison."

"Which friend?"

"The witchy one."

"She's in jail. What would she have to do with this?"

"She got out on bail this morning," Rooster said with a grin.

"If it was poison," I said when Rooster had driven off in his Crown Victoria, "anyone could have done it at any time."

"Whoever it is likes to plan ahead," Tobias said. "Messing with the EpiPen, poisoning... my instinct says that's what happened to José."

"Not a crime of passion, then."

"That kind of takes the Houston woman out of it, doesn't it?" he pointed out.

"It's a far cry from an electric cattle prod," I admitted. "What I want to know is, why would someone want to kill José?"

"He must have known something," Tobias said. "Which points to something at the ranch."

"Not necessarily," I said. "If José overheard something he shouldn't have, that would be an issue. I got the feeling he didn't want us poking around much, though... maybe you're right." As I spoke, there was another gunshot; Tobias and I both flinched.

"Maybe he was afraid you'd get shot," he pointed out.

"Could be, but I got the impression there was more to it than that."

"Hopefully, we'll get a chance to ask him," Tobias said.

Chapter 14

OPAL GRUBER WAS AT HER desk when I stopped by the sheriff's office with a loaf of pumpkin bread in one hand and a stack of paperbacks in the other. Thankfully, there was no sign of Rooster.

"I heard Serafine got out on bail," I said.

"She sure did," Opal said, adjusting her sparkly black cat necklace and eyeing the pumpkin bread with interest. "She was cozied up with that lawyer from Houston yesterday, and this morning she posted bail. I heard you put them in touch."

"I did," I said. "I brought some pumpkin bread and some paperbacks for her, but since she's flown the coop, you're welcome to them." I knew we shared similar taste in both books.

"That's sweet of you," she said, inspecting the books I set on the desk. "Ooh, Ellery Adams. I love her books. And I love pumpkin bread. I've been trying to watch my waistline lately, but it's part vegetable, right?"

"Of course," I said, grinning. "I had another question, too. Ethan Schenk told me there was a woman named Evelyn who was over at the Whartons' place last week. Created something of a disturbance, I hear."

"You mean she went after him with an electric cattle prod."

"That's what I heard," I told her." I was wondering if

Rooster might have considered her as a suspect?"

"I doubt it," she said. "Let's see here." She riffled through the papers on her desk. "Here it is. Evelyn Crowley. Lives on Branard, in Houston."

"Mind if I take down that address?"

"Go ahead," she said, repeating it as I scrawled it on a pad I found in my purse.

"I may go ahead and get in touch with her."

"I think you should," she said. "Lord knows Rooster's never going to."

"What I don't get," I told her, "is why he thinks it's murder in the first place."

She leaned forward. "I'm not going to say anything, but..." She dug through her papers until she found something that looked like a report, then pushed it off the edge of the desk so it drifted to the floor. "Oops. Could you get that for me?"

"Of course," I said, reaching for the paper and making a move to hand it to her.

"I'm going to refill my coffee," she said, grabbing a coffee cup instead and standing up. "I'll be back in a second." With a wink, she turned and headed down the hallway, leaving me with the report.

I glanced down at it; it was an autopsy report for Bug Wharton.

Cause of death: anaphylactic shock. Likely caused by bee venom. Stapled to it was an e-mail from a medical examiner in Houston. "EpiPen shows signs of tampering. Analysis revealed that it contained bee venom, with only trace amounts of epinephrine."

I blinked and read it a second time. No wonder Bug Wharton had died. Someone had filled his EpiPen with bee venom!

As Opal headed back down the hallway, I put the

report back on her desk, still thinking about it. Serafine had lots of hives; of course she had access to bee venom. Presuming she knew how to get venom out of bees.

"So," I said as Opal put her fresh cup of coffee down on the desk, "did Rooster say anything about someone putting bees into Bug's truck?"

"Not that I've heard," she said. "Why?"

"There was a twist of paper with a dead bee in it on the front seat of his truck when Peter went to get the EpiPen," I told her. "Someone must have put it in there after Bug and Mitch got out of the car, or it would have been squashed."

"Why is that?"

"Because Mitch was in the passenger seat. Quinn and I saw him get out of the truck."

"Did Rooster ask you about that?"

I grinned. "Umm... no. He didn't."

"Why don't I set you up with one of the deputies later on today? You can just come in and say you thought of something and wanted to share it."

"Got it," I told her. "What time?"

She checked her schedule. "Deputy Shames should be here in about an hour. How about three?"

"I'll be back," I told her. "Thanks."

"My pleasure," she said. "We women have to stick together."

I walked out of the sheriff's office and was on my way to my truck, feeling more optimistic about things, when I saw something that froze my blood.

Jed Stadtler was driving by in a massive Chevy pickup truck. He spotted me, and when our eyes met, he tilted his head and tipped an imaginary hat, steel in his eyes, before turning left at the corner—in the direction of the Blue Onion Cafe.

I hurried to my truck and slid into the driver's seat, feeling my heart race. Did Quinn know her abusive ex was in town? What was he doing here, anyway? I put my seat belt on as I reversed out of my parking place, and, a moment later, turned in the direction he was heading, my heart in my throat. Before long, I was at the Blue Onion...just as Jed was creeping past it.

I pulled up in the closest parking space and catapulted myself out of the car and into the cafe, where several startled patrons glanced up at me. I smiled at them and hurried to the kitchen, where Quinn was humming to herself as she put the finishing touches on a loaf of spice bread.

"Jed just drove by the cafe," I said.

Her face drained of color. "What is he doing here?"

"I don't know," I told her. "Do you still have a restraining order?"

"I don't know if it's still in force, but I had one when he attacked me at the farm," she said. "I'm not sure it's going to make any difference. Besides, he must be on parole; if he violates it, doesn't that mean he goes back to jail?"

"All the more reason to make sure you've got one in place," I told her.

"I hate guns," she said, "but sometimes I feel like maybe I should learn how to use one."

"Maybe he's just in town for a visit," I said, although something told me that wasn't the case.

"Maybe you're right," she said. "But thanks for letting me know. I'm glad I have Pip to keep watch over

me," she said. "At least I won't be surprised this time."
She shook herself, like a duck trying to shed water. "So.
I refuse to let him take over my day. What's going on
with you?"

"Oh, you know. Dry well, haunted house, friend suspected of murder... the usual."

"You have a minute to help me frost and cut up
these pumpkin bars?" she asked, pointing to the trays
of rich, orange-looking sheet cake on the counter.

"Of course," I said, inhaling the spicy sweet scent of
the kitchen.

"The recipe is on that card," she said, pointing to an
index card at the end of the counter. "Butter is softening by the sink, and cream cheese is in the fridge."

"Got it," I said, thankful to have a task to do.

"Did you get your stock tanks refilled?" she asked.

"I did, but I'm making zero progress on solving the
problem. At least that problem," I said as I unwrapped
a bar of cream cheese and popped it into the mixer,
then reached for the butter. "I may have made some
progress on what happened to Bug."

"What happened?"

I told her about the cattle prod incident, and my
thoughts on the paper in the front seat of his truck.
"I'm supposed to go back and mention it to one of
the deputies later on today, and I'm thinking of getting
in touch with the woman in Houston. But I still think
Aimee's involved with the Whartons somehow."

"Think it's related?"

"It might be," I said. "But the cattle prod person may
be more likely."

"Why the heck didn't Rooster pursue that?"

"Because he doesn't like Serafine and she's in town,
so he doesn't have to do anything."

"What the heck does he think her motive is?"

"Animal abuse. Plus, she had access to bee venom." I told her about the autopsy report I'd seen.

"Wow," she said. "That takes some doing. How the heck do you get venom from bees, anyway?"

"I don't know. I'm not sure that's a job I'd want."

"Me neither."

We fell silent for a few minutes as I creamed the powdered sugar into the butter and then added cream cheese and vanilla, making a smooth, sweet frosting that would be a wonderful counterpoint to the moist, velvety pumpkin bars. I added a dash of almond extract at the end— Quinn had taught me it was her secret weapon—and then began slathering the frosting onto the moist cake.

I had just frosted the second pan and was moving onto the third when there was a loud bang. I turned around to see Jed Stadtler standing in the kitchen.

"What are you doing here?" Quinn had gone white and backed up against the wall.

"Just being neighborly," Jed said in a smooth, preda-tory tone that made my hackles rise. I grabbed a rolling pin off the counter and moved closer to Quinn. I knew she was testing for her black belt soon, but Jed still towered over her. "It's been a while, baby. I just wanted to see how you're doing. I've missed you."

"Please leave," she said in a firm voice.

"That's not very friendly," he said in a wheedling tone that made my stomach turn. "I was hoping we'd let bygones be bygones. After all, this town isn't very big. Might as well kiss and make up."

"Leave," she repeated, only without the please. "Now. Or I'm calling the police."

"You think Rooster's going to come to your rescue?" he asked, a half smile playing on his handsome face. He took a step toward my friend, and she sidled away. "Not that he needs to. I've changed, Quinn."

She swallowed hard, but said nothing. I could practically smell the fear coming off her; I was sure he could, too.

"All that stuff before? I see how wrong I was. You and I were meant to be together."

"Get out," she said in a low voice. "You aren't welcome here."

He reached over and grabbed a freshly frosted cinnamon roll from the rack by the door. He took a slow bite and chewed. "I always did like your cooking." He grabbed two more and then sauntered to the door. "I've missed you, Quinn. I'll see you around. Very soon."

Jed left the way he'd come. When the door shut behind him, I scurried over and turned the deadbolt, then watched out the window as he sauntered over to his truck and got in. He gunned the engine a couple of times, then peeled out of his parking place, leaving a cloud of exhaust in his wake.

I turned to Quinn, who had sagged against the wall, and hurried to her side. "Are you okay?"

"No," she said. "I can't believe he just walked in here like that."

"I think you need to make sure that restraining order is still in place."

"I guess I do," she said. "Once he was put away, I just didn't worry about it."

"I think you're going to have to start worrying again, unfortunately." I squeezed her shoulder. "Do you need a hug?"

She nodded, and as I put my arms around her, she burst into tears.

"I've got your back," I said.

"I know," she said, wiping her eyes. "I'm just not sure it will be enough."

"You can come and stay with me if you want," I offered.

"It didn't stop him last time."

"I know. I just thought not being alone..."

She pulled back and wiped her eyes. "I've got Pip. Besides, I refuse to let that man dictate how I live my life. He's caused me enough pain already."

"I just don't like the idea of you being here alone," I repeated. "It's nice to have someone who has your back. In fact, I'm happy to stay here for a few days."

"No," she said. "Thanks, but I've got Pip."

I nodded. "If you change your mind..."

"I'll tell you," she said, and the subject was closed.

Opal was right about the deputy; when I walked into the station at three, she was standing in the front office, talking with Opal.

"You've met Deputy Shames, right?" Opal asked, indicating the fit young woman standing next to the desk.

"No, I haven't," I said. "I'm Lucy Resnick. And I'm glad you're here. Quinn's ex, Jed Stadtler, walked into the kitchen of the Blue Onion and threatened Quinn today."

Opal's eyes hardened. "He just can't leave that poor woman alone, can he?"

"She doesn't want to report it, but if you could have someone keep an eye on the Blue Onion, I'd really appreciate it."

"Doesn't she have a restraining order?" Deputy Shames asked. She had long brown hair scraped back into a ponytail, dark eyes, and an air of quiet competence about her. Where Rooster's uniform frequently sported barbecue stains, hers looked like she'd pressed it before getting dressed that morning. "That might be a parole violation."

"It would be, if it hasn't expired," Opal said.

"If it's still in force, we can arrest him. If it isn't, she needs to get the judge to renew it," the deputy informed me.

"How do I find that out?"

"If she doesn't still have a copy, she'll have to go to the court to find out," Opal said. "And it may be in the terms of his parole. I'll look in to it."

"Thanks," I said. "By the way," I added, addressing the deputy, "I forgot to mention it at the time, but there was a twist of paper with a dead bee in it on the front seat of Bug Wharton's truck. It wasn't crushed, so it seems to me that someone must have put it in the car after Bug and Mitch got out of it."

"Is that in evidence?" Deputy Shames asked Opal.

"It is, but I don't think Rooster's done anything with it."

"Can we make sure we get it checked for fingerprints?" she asked. "It may be nothing, but it's best to be thorough."

"Happy to," Opal said.

"I'm impressed," I said. "When did you join the force?"

"Six months ago," she said. "I finished the academy

in Houston and they assigned me here."

"Quite a change from Houston," I said. "I used to live there, too; I was a reporter."

"What brought you to Buttercup?" the deputy asked.

I smiled. "My grandmother's farm. And the so-called quiet life."

Opal snorted. "Shoulda stayed in Houston."

"Also, I heard there was an incident out at the Whartons' place a couple of days before Bug died. Do you know if Rooster's got that in mind?"

"I don't—he's managing the case—but I'll see what I can find out."

"I've got the lady's info right here," Opal said. "If you want, I can get you the address."

Deputy Shames sucked air in through her teeth. "I don't want to step on any toes. I'm low woman on the totem pole around here."

"I get it," I said, thinking a trip to Houston might be in my upcoming plans. "Do you know if Rooster's looking at any other suspects?"

She shook her head. "From what I hear, he's decided he's got the perp."

"What do you think?" I asked.

She glanced at the door and then at Opal before answering. "I think there may be more to the story than he's aware of," she said diplomatically.

That made two of us.

"He's sure it's murder?" I asked, as if I hadn't seen the autopsy report.

She nodded. "It's pretty clear it was, actually."

"Why does he think it's Serafine, if you don't mind my asking?"

"Because of that blowup they had at the Witches' Ball," Deputy Shames said. "Practically the entire town saw it, and then she threw his cup into the fire."

"Are they thinking she poisoned the mead? If so, the whole town could have been poisoned."

"Only if they were allergic to bees."

"Did anyone else have a reaction?"

She shook her head. "Of course, she could have poisoned just his cup."

"I was thinking... the paper said he died from anaphylaxis, right?"

The deputy nodded.

"Maybe it wasn't anything in the cup. If I'm right, and someone put that bee in Bug's truck after he and his brother parked, then it might not be a bad idea to find out if Serafine ever left the cauldron. When we walked into the ball, right after Bug did, she was there serving mead; she was still there when we left the fortune-teller's booth and saw the argument with Bug."

"How long was that?"

"Not long at all. Fifteen, twenty minutes."

"Assuming the bee is the source of the allergic reaction—and that's not a given, because she burned the cup—if she stayed at the cauldron the whole time, there's no way she could have put the bee in the truck."

"Exactly." Of course, I knew the EpiPen was the likely cause of death, but there must have been something that sparked the allergic reaction. "Most of the town was there; if she'd left, someone would have seen her.

Deputy Shames's eyes brightened. "Was anyone else working in that general area?"

"The fortune-teller," I said. "Aimee. She was facing the cauldron while she was working."

"Who else?"

"I don't know," I said, "but just about all of Buttercup

was there. If she left, someone would have seen her; with that gigantic black hat, she was hard to miss."

"Unless she took it off," Opal pointed out.

"Maybe," I said. "Think Serafine has a list of everyone who attended? Maybe we could ask folks what they saw."

"That sounds like a lot of work. I'm not even on the case."

"I could do some asking around and let you know if I hear anything."

"It's not really part of police procedure," she said.

"I know. But arresting a woman and not considering other suspects is also not part of police procedure. And I'm not crazy about the idea of an innocent young woman going to prison for a crime she didn't commit."

"Point taken," she said.

"Lucy here was an investigative reporter in Houston," Opal piped up. "She knows what she's doing."

I smiled. "Thanks for the vote of confidence. If it's okay with you, I'll see what I can find out."

"You can poke around, I guess."

"Also... any way to run a background check on both of the Whartons—and the Houston woman?"

"I'll see what turns up," she agreed. "But it's an off-duty, unofficial kind of thing. If Rooster finds out I'm nosing around in his case..."

"He won't like it one bit," Opal said. "We'll have to be quiet about it. But he's got it wrong so many dad-gum times, I don't know that we've got a choice."

"Thanks," I said. "I know in my gut she's not the one who did it." But I still wasn't quite sure about her sister. I almost asked Opal to do a background check on her, but something held me back.

I wanted to do a little more poking around on my own. I had a bad feeling Aimee was into something her sister wouldn't like. I just hoped it didn't involve murder.

Chapter 15

EVELYN CROWLEY LIVED IN AN older area of Houston, a mix of old houses and shopping centers; with no zoning, Houston was always a grab bag.

The address was on Branard Street; it was a cute brick cottage with an arched front door and one lone pumpkin for autumnal decor. A few bedraggled rosebushes flanked the front porch, and the grass didn't look like it had been mowed in several months, but the house had potential.

I got out and walked up the bedraggled path to the front door, still trying to decide what I was going to say. I wasn't going to lead with "Did you murder Bug Wharton?"

I'd figure out something. Assuming she was home, I thought, as I pushed the glowing doorbell button. Fortunately, I seemed to be in luck; a moment later, I heard the tap-tap of high-heeled shoes on hardwood floors, and then the door opened.

"I don't need any cleaning products," she said, and started to close the door.

"I'm not here to sell you anything," I replied, and put my foot in the door, an old trick from my days as a reporter. "Do you know what happened to Bug Wharton?"

She blinked at me. She was a tall woman, around forty-five, in a fashionable shift dress with a chunky bead necklace. She jutted out her chin. "I don't really care what happened to Bug Wharton."

"He's dead," I said.

Her tan face paled and her chin dropped. Evidently she did care what happened to Bug Wharton. And unless she was a very good actress, the news was a surprise. "What? What happened? Was it a heart attack? I told him he needed to cut back on the brisket..."

"It wasn't a heart attack," I said. "Can I come in?"

"Of course," she said. "I'm so sorry. I'm just... so shocked. Come in, come in," she said, and I followed her into the little house. The inside was tidier than the outside, although the place could use some updating. The front hall was tiled in what looked like frosted gingersnaps, and yellowed grass paper covered the walls. I followed her into the small living room, which was furnished with a sagging green sofa and two mismatched leather armchairs. She gestured to the couch, then sat down across from me, hugging herself. "I can't believe he's gone," she said, her eyes tearing up.

"I'm sorry to surprise you like that. I'm Lucy Resnick. I live in Buttercup, not far from the Whartons'."

"I'm Evelyn, but I'm guessing you figured that out or you wouldn't be here." She swiped at her eyes. "What happened to him?"

"He died under suspicious circumstances," I told her. "I was wondering if you had any idea who might have wished him ill."

"Suspicious circumstances?"

"Anaphylactic shock," I clarified.

"And they think someone did that to him?" she asked. "Oh my God. I can't believe it. Someone killed him?"

"I'm not totally privy to what happened, but that seems to be the theory." I decided not to tell her that Serafine was in custody. "Did you know Bug well?"

"Bug," she said, shaking her head. "What a stupid nickname. I don't know why he couldn't be Buddy, or Bubba, or something more normal. I always called him Bruce."

"Bruce?"

She nodded. "It sounds so much better than Bug. Although I guess I won't have to say his name any-more, will I?" She dissolved into tears again. I waited until the sobs had subsided before continuing.

"You were close, weren't you?" I asked in my softest voice.

"Yeah," she said, reaching for a tissue and dabbing at her eyes. "It was a roller-coaster ride we were on, that's for sure. I just broke up with him last week, and now... this."

"I'm so sorry," I told her.

"I guess I figured we weren't getting back together again after what happened, but now... I guess that option really is off the table, isn't it?" She sounded bereft.

"How long were you together?"

"Well, I don't know how long we were actually together—it was on-again, off-again—but we started dating over two years ago," she told me. "When we were together, it was awesome, but it never lasted long."

I'd heard of tumultuous relationships, but never one that had involved electric cattle prods. "I understand you two had a falling-out last week. What was that about?"

She gave me a sheepish look. "You heard about it, eh?"

"Buttercup is a small town," I reminded her.

She sighed. "I guess so. So, you heard about... the incident?"

"The cattle prod?"

She blushed through her tears. "It was a tough night."

"I hope you don't mind my asking," I said gently, "but what happened?"

"I found out he was seeing someone else," she said, and burst into tears all over again. "We were supposed to be getting married in June. And then... I saw his phone, and there were messages from this other woman. I was so mad I just... well, you know."

"I know," I said. "I've been there, too. I hate to ask... but do you know who the other woman was?"

"No," she said. "But whoever it was was talking about meeting late at night, and how excited she was about it. I threw his phone in the pond. I have a bit of a temper. It can be a problem sometimes."

Enough of a problem to kill him? I wondered. But poisoning him with an EpiPen seemed more of a premeditated type of thing. "Did he have a lot of allergies?" I asked.

"Bees, mainly," she said. "He got stung last year and spent a week in the hospital. He wasn't at all afraid of those stupid animals he imported, but he wouldn't get anywhere near a beehive."

"How did he decide to open an exotic game ranch, anyway?" I asked.

"He had a thing for hunting," she said. "The bigger the better. He was talking about getting some big cats in, but I talked him out of it."

"Big cats? Like lions?"

"Tigers, I think," she said. "They were super-expensive, though. And dangerous."

I'll bet, I thought, thinking about the wounded oryx. "Did he go ahead with it?"

"Thankfully not. Some places feed them frozen guinea pigs." She shuddered. "No, carnivores are scary."

"When was he talking about it?"

"A month or two ago," she said. "Knew some guy in Katy with a bunch of tiger cubs, I think. I hate the whole idea of raising animals just to kill them, but endangered tigers?"

"So, you knew him before he bought the ranch?"

"I did," she said. "He was still working."

"Where did he work?" I asked, making a mental note of it.

"Some tech company," she said. "I never got the details. He did really well when they sold it."

"Why do you say that?"

"He told me. A couple of years ago, he was living in an apartment in Dallas and driving a beater car. Now he's got... or had... a huge luxury ranch. I've heard those tech companies make a lot of money when they go public."

"Must be nice," I said, although I couldn't imagine working for a tech company. "Were things going well with the ranch?"

"It was going okay, but I don't think it was the moneymaker he expected it to be. I think the drought kind of made it more expensive than he thought it would be to keep all those animals."

"I can believe that," I said. With the drought, temperatures had soared the past few months. "Did he ever talk about selling it?"

"No," she said, "but he was looking at alternate income streams. He told me once if he could hold on until December, he'd be okay."

"What was going to happen in December?"

She shrugged. "I don't know. Maybe some investor or something." She grew teary again. "I just can't believe he's gone."

"I'm so sorry," I said. "Was the night you had the argument at the ranch the last time you saw him?"

She sniffled and nodded, but cut her eyes away. "Yes. Yes, it was."

"So, you broke off the engagement?" I asked, although I noticed she was still wearing a silver ring with a big diamond on her left hand.

"It was still... in process," she said awkwardly. "Look, I've got an appointment in a half hour."

"I'll go," I said. "But one more question: Were there any Buttercup folks out at the ranch, ever?"

"What do you mean? Like, working there?"

"That, or visiting," I said.

"Well, he hired some guy named Jack or Jeb or something to help out with the animals a week or two ago," she said.

"Jed?" I asked, my hackles rising.

"That's it," she said. "Tall guy. Good-looking."

"Right," I said, feeling my stomach curdle. "Anyone else?"

"I saw one of those hippie women from that mead place a couple of times," she said. "I think she might have been sweet on Mitch."

"Oh?" I asked. "Why do you say that?"

"I was walking, and I caught them kissing down by the creek."

"How long ago?"

"Two weeks ago," she said. "I cleared my throat and they jumped away from each other like they were burned."

Interesting. "Did Bug and Mitch get along?"

"They did, for the most part, but I know Mitch was worried about money. Bug didn't like his plans, though. Said they were too risky."

"In what way?"

She shrugged. "I didn't pay attention to that stuff. Some scheme of Mitch's, I guess. I didn't get involved. He probably spent too much at one of those riverboat casinos he likes to go to."

"Riverboat casinos?"

She narrowed her eyes at me and crossed her arms. "Why do you care about the Whartons so much?"

It was my turn to evade. "Habit, I guess"

Evelyn stood up. "I probably shouldn't have talked to you so much," she said.

"I'm glad you did," I said. "One last question," I added as she led me to the door. "Was it common knowledge that Bug was allergic to bees?"

She shook her head. "He didn't talk about it. Viewed it as some kind of weakness."

Which meant whoever had filled that EpiPen was close enough to Bug to know he had a deadly Achilles' heel. "What kind of work do you do, by the way?"

"Who, me? I'm a nurse practitioner. That's how Bug and I met, actually. He asked me out after an appointment." The memory brought back a rush of emotion, and she dabbed at her eyes as she opened the door for me.

Before stepping out, I fished a card out of my back pocket. "If you're ever in Buttercup, feel free to stop by," I said.

She studied the card. "You have a farm stand?"

"No," I said, "but I have plenty of jam around the place, and fresh veggies. I'm happy to share."

"Thanks," she said. "But I have no reason to go back to Buttercup. Ever."

A moment later I was on the front porch, the card still in my hand, wondering about Evelyn Crawley... and whether her grief was quite as genuine as it had seemed.

Houston felt as far away as China when I drove past Buttercup's Town Square two hours later. To my relief, there were no goats or wayward cows nosing at the chrysanthemums flanking the Town Hall, and the winter veggie starts and pansies on display in front of the Red and White were equally unmolested by Dewberry Farm's prodigal livestock. Autumn displays decorated the storefronts; Fannie's Antiques was filled with red and gold leaves and vintage fall linens, and the Blue Onion's window featured loaves of gourds and pumpkins interspersed with gorgeous braided loaves and the pumpkin bars I had frosted at the cafe. I stopped to tell Quinn what I'd learned about Jed, but the doors were locked and she didn't answer her door, so I called and left a message instead.

A few minutes later, I bumped over the railroad tracks, waving at Bessie Mae, and headed not to Dewberry Farm but toward the Honeyed Moon winery. I had a few questions for Aimee, and I wasn't in the mood to be lied to.

Aimee was walking out of the winery's barn when I pulled up the long driveway. She squinted into the sunshine and gave me a half-hearted wave.

"Any news?" she asked when I got out of the truck.

"Sort of," I said, closing the door behind me. "What

was going on between you and Mitch Wharton?"

"Nothing," she said, too hurriedly.

"You were kissing him down by the creek a week or two ago, from what I hear. And I saw your car at the ranch earlier this week. That doesn't sound like nothing to me."

"It's none of your business what's going on with me."

"I disagree," I said. "If you want me to find out who killed Bug Wharton, I think you're going to have to tell me everything."

Her mocha-colored skin turned a shade paler, and she crossed her arms. "I don't see how my personal life has anything to do with what happened to that jerk."

I sighed. "Look, Aimee. Your sister went to jail for murdering the brother of a man I think you were secretly seeing. I'm sorry, but that means there's some connection there I don't know about, and if I'm supposed to find out the truth, you have to tell me everything you know."

She said nothing, her full lips a thin line.

"If you don't tell me, I'll have to start asking around. And Buttercup is a small town. You may think you were clever enough to hide whatever was going on, but I assure you, someone in this town knows more than you think they know." I paused, watching her face, which remained impassive. "Tobias and I heard you and Mitch arguing at the ranch the other day." Her nostrils flared slightly, and I thought I detected a flicker of fright in her eyes. "What are the odds that Serafine—or Rooster Kocurek—doesn't know something was going on between you and Mitch?"

I let that sink in for a moment before continuing. "You can tell me your side of the story, or I can find it out from somebody else. Your choice."

The silence seemed to stretch into the next county, but I resisted the urge to break it. In my role as an investigative reporter, I'd learned that silence was an excellent tool to use when asking difficult questions.

Finally, she sighed, dropping her arms. "Okay," she said. "But I need a glass of mead. Or something."

She turned on a booted heel and headed toward the farmhouse she and Serafine shared, and I followed quietly.

The inside of the house was as cozy as it looked on the outside, with refinished floors and fresh white batten-board walls. I followed her through the dining room into the kitchen, which was decorated with colorful Mexican pottery and small pieces of folk art. She gestured for me to sit at the small kitchen table, then pulled a bottle of mead from the refrigerator and filled two jam jars, sliding one across the tile-topped table to me before plunking herself down on the chair across from me.

I took a sip of the mead, which was honey sweet and had the tantalizing aroma of spices. Aimee, on the other hand, downed hers in one go and then reached for the bottle, refilling her glass. She'd finished half of it before slamming her glass down on the table and looking at me.

"All right," she said in a flat voice. "What do you want to know?"

I took another sip of mead before answering in a calm voice. "How long have you been seeing Mitch?" I asked.

"About two months," she said, dropping her eyes to her glass.

"Why did you feel you had to keep it a secret?"

She looked up at me, blinking. "Seriously? My sister

would have killed me if she knew I was going out with one of the Whartons!"

"How did you end up meeting him, anyway?" I asked.

"It was funny," she said, her eyes getting a bit dreamy. "We were both at the same gas station in La Grange. I noticed him right away... there was just something about him."

"Did you start talking then?"

She laughed. "I was about to drive off without my gas cap on. He flagged me down and we started talking... it didn't take long to figure out we were both from Buttercup. And when we figured out who we were..." She let out a husky laugh. "We could tell it was going to be a Romeo-and-Juliet kind of thing. That's why our first date was in Houston."

"You drove all the way to Houston for a date?"

"I did," she said, ducking her head. "It was worth it, too. We went dancing."

"It sounds like you two are pretty well-matched."

"Yeah," she said. "For a right-wing conservative rancher and a liberal hippie witch."

"Opposites do attract. So, what happened?"

"It was too hard to keep it going, I guess. With all the secrecy. And he was kind of... well, controlling."

That didn't sound good. "Why did you feel the need to keep it secret, anyway?" I asked.

She sighed. "I think neither of us really felt like we were in charge of our own lives, you know? I mean, Bug ran the ranch, and I'm only here because Serafine invited me; the place is hers, not mine."

"So, you were afraid they'd cast you out?"

She nodded. "They were both so... strident about each other," she said. "If I didn't know Serafine had such a good heart, I'd be afraid she did kill Bug Wharton. She hated him that much. And Bug thought Serafine was a total faker... which she definitely isn't." Aimee bit her lip. "It was almost like he was worried she was going to dig up something he didn't want dug up."

"Like what?"

She shrugged. "At any rate," she said, getting up, "you know everything I know. I've got chores to do."

"Thanks for being honest with me," I said as I walked to the door. "If you think of anything else, let me know."

"I doubt I will, but thanks anyway," she said dismissively.

Chapter 16

"ANY WORD FROM JED?" I asked when I got to the Blue Onion the next morning. After my visit with Aimee, I'd gone home and made several batches of soap and some candles; Christmas would be coming soon, and I wanted to have plenty of merchandise. I had signed up to do a few markets in Austin; I was hoping they would be profitable.

Quinn was elbows deep in a bowl of dough. She was pale, and there were dark circles under her eyes; I hadn't seen her look so rattled in a long time.

"I'm not sure," she said. "Pip growled a few times last night, and I thought I heard something from downstairs, but I didn't see him."

"I don't like that," I said. "What's going on with the restraining order?"

"I haven't heard back yet," she said.

"Are you sure you don't want to come out and stay with me?"

"He found me there, too, remember?" she asked.

"And we dealt with him together, too," I reminded her.

"I hear he got a job at the game ranch. Why would he come back to Buttercup? I swear, that man just wants to ruin my life."

"Well, let's make sure that doesn't happen, then." I

grabbed an apron.

"Are you still planning on having us over for Halloween?" she asked.

"I am," I said.

"I'll bring pumpkin bars," she said. "But now I'm nervous," she said. "What if Jed shows up?"

"At least you won't have to face him alone," I pointed out. "What can I do to help you prepare?"

"If you'll measure out those nuts and mix them with cinnamon and sugar, that would be great," she said, pointing to a recipe book on the counter.

"The offer is open," I said. "You can stay with me anytime."

"I'll think about it," she said, but she didn't say another word about it. I worried as I watched my friend worked. I knew she was determined not to let Jed upend her life, but he was doing it anyway.

It just didn't seem fair.

I got back to the farm late. Evening was falling, but despite rumors that a Blue Norther with possible rainfall was headed our way, there was still no sign of a storm when I headed out to do my chores. It was a relief to have the stock tank filled, at least for now. I'd rigged up a pump with about twelve extension cords and attached it to a series of soaker hoses. I turned on the pump and checked to make sure water was moving, then headed over toward Blossom, Peony, and the goats.

I knew right away that something was wrong.

Instead of standing by the fence, waiting for treats, the goats were huddled in the corner of the enclosure closest to the barn, bleating nervously. Blossom and Peony were close by; as I watched, Blossom tossed her head and sidled up next to her daughter. They were obviously spooked.

"What's up?" I asked, scanning the area as I hurried back to the stock tank to turn off the pump. I didn't see anything, but as my eyes swept the far end of the pasture, a low growl reached my ears. All the hair on my body stood on end.

"It's okay," I told them in a calm voice, thankful I'd left Chuck in the house. "Let's get everyone inside." I let myself into the pasture and they followed me straight to the barn, pushing past one another to get in. Blossom and Peony joined them a moment later, and once I got everyone into stalls, I stepped back outside, wondering—yet again—if I should get over my squeamishness involving firearms and invest in some kind of gun.

I closed the barn door behind me and stood, listening. Other than the bursts of song of the wind chimes behind the farmhouse, the only sound was the wind soughing through the grass, and a low moan as it curled around the edges of the barn roof. The sky was streaked with sunset colors: cobalt blue, tangerine orange, and streaks of fuchsia.

After five minutes of scanning the peach orchard and the tangle of brush and small trees down by the creek, I was about to turn back and start milking the goats when I heard it again.

It was coming from a small cedar break about fifty feet away, and the sound was chilling. With one hand on the barn door, I peered into the dark green branches. I caught a glimpse of movement; a moment later, a large, shadowy creature slid from one tree to another. I wasn't sure what it was, but it didn't look like anything I'd ever seen before. Behind me, the goats shuffled nervously. I watched for a minute more, not sure if I was hoping to see it again or not, before closing the barn door and hurrying to the house. Chuck was upset, too; his hackles were up as he stood at the door, and his chunky frame vibrated with a low growl. I closed the door behind me and headed for the phone.

Tobias picked up on the second ring. "I think I saw whatever it is that's been attacking the animals," I told him.

"Is it still there?"

"I don't know. I put everyone in the barn and I'm in the house with Chuck."

"I'll be right over," he said. "Don't go outside, but keep an eye out."

I hung up and joined Chuck at the door, peering through the window at the copse of trees where I'd seen the creature. What was it? I wondered, wishing I'd gotten a better glimpse. The sun continued to fall behind the trees, darkening the world, as I watched and waited. When the phone rang again, Chuck and I both jumped.

It was Quinn. "I hate to ask, but I've seen Jed circle the building four times tonight, and Pip's kind of freaked out. Do you mind if I stay with you tonight?"

"Of course," I said. "Did you call the police?"

"I did, but they're short-staffed tonight."

"Come on over," I said. "I think I just saw the chupacabra, or whatever it is that's been stalking the local farm animals. I could use the company."

"You know, I'm starting to rethink my position on guns," Quinn said.

"We'll talk about it when you get here," I said.

"I'm on my way."

As I hung up the phone, headlights flashed at the end of the driveway. For a horrible moment, I thought it might be Jed, but I soon recognized Tobias's truck.

"Stay here," I told Chuck, and went out to meet him.

"Any more sightings?" he asked as he climbed out of the truck.

"No," I told him. "I watched at the window and didn't see anything, but Chuck is still rattled. Quinn's on her way, too; Jed's been circling her place tonight, and Rooster says he doesn't have enough staff to post a guard."

"Lovely," he said as he retrieved what looked like a rifle from a rack in the back of the truck.

"You're going to shoot it?" I asked, surprised.

"It's a tranquilizer gun," he clarified, handing me a flashlight; dusk had slid into darkness. "Where did you see it?"

"Over here," I said, and headed across the bleached grass toward the shadowy trees where I'd seen the creature, Tobias at my shoulder. The wind whispered through the grass, and somewhere, a branch cracked. We both froze; the trees loomed ominously, like an enchanted wood in a fairy tale. Was there a supernatural creature crouched in there among the scrub oaks and cedars?

"I should have brought a flashlight," I whispered as Tobias raised the tranquilizer gun, scanning the area. After a moment, he took another step forward. As he moved, headlights glared at the end of the driveway. As the beams of light swept across the copse, a pair of eyes glowed.

"There it is!" I hissed, but Tobias had been distracted by the headlights. There was a rustle in the copse, and

I caught a glimpse of something large loping away before it was swallowed by the darkness.

"What was that?" I asked.

"I don't know," he said, "but it didn't move like a coyote." As he spoke, Quinn pulled up next to Tobias's truck; a moment later, she opened the door, and Pip bounded out.

"Hold him!" I said, too late; he was already on his way toward us. I didn't know what was in the trees, but I didn't want Pip to tangle with whatever it was, so I crouched down and called to the black dog. "Come here, boy!" I cooed, relieved when he trotted over and nuzzled my leg. I grabbed his collar just in time; there was a breeze from the vicinity of the trees, and Pip's lithe body erupted into a growl.

"Let's get back to the house," Tobias said.

"What's going on?" Quinn asked when she spotted us.

"We saw something in the trees," Tobias explained. "Something's been preying on livestock around town recently; we were checking it out." Pip was still growling, trying to twist out of my grasp.

"Whatever it is, Pip sure doesn't like it," Quinn said. "Is everyone safe in the barn?"

I nodded. "They were right by the door, anxious to get in; whatever it was really spooked them. All kinds of prowlers out tonight, it seems... I'm so sorry Jed was bothering you."

"Is Rooster doing anything about it?" Tobias asked.

"No," Quinn replied as she opened the door to the farmhouse. Chuck attempted to squirt out of the house, but Quinn grabbed him before he could get off the porch. The dogs growled and barked as we shepherded them inside to safety.

When the door was shut safely behind us, I turned to Quinn. "Why doesn't he have someone keeping tabs on you?"

"Says they're short-staffed, as usual." Her mouth twisted into a wry smile, and she looked at Tobias. "I heard you saved some guy at the ranch, by the way."

"I don't know if I saved him, but he was in pretty bad shape when we found him," Tobias replied.

"Do you know if he's doing okay?" I asked.

"Word is he seems to be recovering. They posted someone to watch his room at the hospital; that's why they didn't have staff to keep tabs on my place."

"You're always welcome here." I gave Quinn a hug. "But I don't know what we're going to do if he shows up with a gun."

"I'll stay," Tobias volunteered. "And if worse comes to worst, I have this." He held up the tranquilizer gun.

"I'd love that," I told him. "I think we'd both sleep better. But are you sure?"

"I forwarded calls from the hospital to my phone," he told us. "If anyone needs me, they know where to find me."

"I'll heat up something for dinner, then. I've got a lasagna in the freezer. I'll just pop it in the oven, and we'll see if we can rustle up enough greens for a salad."

"Still no word from Lenny, eh?" he asked.

I grimaced. "Not a peep."

"We'll figure something out," he said. "But let's not worry about that tonight."

"No well water, Jed Stadtler on the loose, my friend charged with homicide, a weird predator stalking my livestock, and a murderer probably on the loose in Buttercup. What could I possibly be worried about?"

"Don't forget the haunted house," Quinn chimed in.

I sighed. "How could I forget?"

"Did you ever get that diary to Maria?" Quinn asked.

"I did," I said as I rummaged through the freezer and pulled out a pan of lasagna. "She spent over an hour poking around to see if there were any other secret caches in the house, but I don't think she found anything."

"Any ghostly appearances while she was there?" Quinn asked.

I shook my head and turned the oven on. "I think she was a little disappointed."

"Maybe the ghost wanted someone to find the diary," Quinn suggested. "It could be that's what it was trying to say."

"You really think the house is haunted?" Tobias asked.

"I didn't see any loose shutters," I pointed out as I tucked the lasagna into the oven. I stood up and peered out the darkening windows. "Do you think it's safe to go get some salad makings?"

"I'll go," Tobias announced.

"I'll go with you," I told him. "That way we'll have each other's backs."

"I don't know. Fresh salad is good, but it's not worth being mauled by..."

"...A chupacabra?" I finished.

"No such thing," Tobias asserted yet again. "But there are mountain lions."

"Good thing you have a tranquilizer gun, then. Besides, the dogs have settled down."

He glanced at Chuck and Pip, who were still agitated, but no longer growling, then opened and closed his mouth as if he were about to tell me no, but thought better of it. "All right," he said. "But stay close."

Quinn corralled the dogs as I grabbed a flashlight

and a basket and headed for the back door with Tobias behind me. Together, we headed out into the darkness. "This way," I told him, leading him toward where I'd planted rows of greens. "I need to thin the arugula anyway."

"Fine, but we should hurry up about it," Tobias said. "I don't feel like shooting a mountain lion tonight."

"I'm glad," I told him. "I wouldn't want to hang out with someone who wanted to shoot a mountain lion."

As Tobias stood guard, I used a flashlight to find the row of arugula and then bent down to pluck enough to fill the basket. I was halfway down the row when there was a low, deep growl from somewhere close to the barn.

I stood up and whirled around, shining the flashlight in the direction of the sound. I caught a flash of eyeshine, then a quick, sinuous movement as something darted around the corner of the barn. The goats bleated anxiously from inside, and the dogs began barking and yipping behind the farmhouse door.

"We're going back inside," Tobias said, shouldering the gun, and I didn't argue. "Stay behind me."

I did, happily, as we hustled from the garden to the house. "Are you sure the barn is locked up tight?" he asked as we entered the warm pool of light glowing from the kitchen windows. I kept shining the light behind us, just in case whatever it was decided we looked tasty, but there was no sign of the creature.

"Now you're making me doubt myself," I said, "but I don't want to check. Besides, if I hadn't, wouldn't that... whatever it was already have gotten in?"

"Probably," he admitted as I pulled open the kitchen door.

"Are you okay?" Quinn asked as we burst into the

kitchen. "The dogs went nuts again."

"We saw it," I told her. "By the barn."

"What do you think it is?" she asked.

"I didn't get a good look, but it's definitely a predator," Tobias said. "It didn't have the look of a wolf, but I don't think it was a mountain lion, either."

"Why not?"

"It moved differently, somehow," he said. "I don't know what it was. I do know one thing, though."

"What?"

"It wasn't a chupacabra, because they don't exist."

After a few minutes, the dogs settled down. When Chuck reclaimed his spot next to the woodstove in the kitchen, Tobias stood up. "I'm going to go check to make sure the barn is secure."

"Want company?" I asked as I picked roots off the baby arugula.

"No," he said shortly. "I'll be back in a few."

Quinn and I watched as he headed out the front door. I abandoned the arugula, feeling anxious as he opened the gate and headed toward the barn, the gun at the ready.

He checked the first barn door and had rounded the building to check the back when the dogs erupted behind us.

I cracked the door open. "Tobias, watch out!" I yelled. He rounded the barn a moment later, paused, and then started running... but not toward the house.

"Where are you going?"

"Fire!" he yelled. "Call the fire department!"

Chapter 17

"I'LL CALL," QUINN SAID AND raced for the phone as I bolted out of the farmhouse. The smell of smoke was on the air; when I turned, I saw flames leaping down by the dry creek. Which was downhill from us. Which meant the flames would soon be rushing toward the farmhouse.

My throat turned dry, and I caught a movement on the other side of the creek. It wasn't an animal; it was a person; I caught a quick glimpse of a face, and then it was gone.

I grabbed Tobias's arm. "There's someone down there."

He surveyed the flame-lit area. "I don't see anything. Are you sure it's not the mountain lion?"

"I saw a face," I said.

"No time to chase it down now," he pointed out.

"I know. We need to get the hose and pump water from the stock tank," I replied. "It's not much, but it's something. If you'll grab the hose, I'll go get the pump going."

"I'll put the dogs in the truck," Quinn said. "What do you want me to do about the animals?"

"If it gets too close, open the barn and the gates," I told her. "At least they can escape."

"What about whatever was out there?"

"We'll just have to hope the fire will scare it off." I paused. "And grab my grandmother's cookbook from the shelf." If I lost the house, at least I'd have something to remember her by.

"Got it," she said as we ran out the door.

By the time we got the water going, the fire had advanced and was about fifteen feet from my peach orchard. As Tobias tried to wet down the dry grass ahead of the advancing flames, I ran to get a bucket and filled it. Despite our best efforts, the fire was spreading.

"We don't have enough water!" Tobias yelled when the first peach tree caught fire. I winced as the little tree flamed, then blackened, and glanced back toward the farmhouse. My grandparents' home had survived for more than a hundred years. Would this be the end of it?

At that moment, headlights flashed behind us; the pumper truck came roaring up the driveway, then bumped down the pasture toward us. The fire brigade had arrived.

Peter and Ethan swung down from the truck. "Get to safety," Peter ordered us as they worked to get the hose detached from the truck. A moment later, a solid spray of water had slowed the fire's advance on the orchard. Unfortunately, there was only one truck, and a snake of fire was slithering toward the barn.

"I've got it," Tobias said when I pointed it out, and hurried over with the hose. I stamped out some of the flames as he watered the dry grass between the fire and the barn; with luck, it would at least slow it down. I turned back to watch Peter and Ethan battle the flames. They'd saved the peach orchard, but another line of flame was hurrying up the pasture.

"It's all going to go up, isn't it?" I asked Tobias.

He squeezed my arm. "It might be time to go open the gates."

My stomach clenched as I ran to the barn. Would I be able to get them out in time? Between the skulking predator that had recently been snuffling around and the smell of smoke, would they even come to me?

I opened the gate and hurried to the barn door, unlocking it and throwing it open.

"Come on, girls," I cajoled, but everyone was huddled at the back of the barn, the whites visible around their terrified eyes. "Let's go," I said in my softest voice, taking a step forward, but they just pressed against the back of the barn. For the first time, I began to panic. I couldn't bear to lose them to the fire. But how was I going to get them out of here in time? Even if I managed to rope the spooked animals, was I strong enough to get them to the door?

I grabbed a length of rope from a peg by the door and hurried to the closest goat, which happened to be Hot Lips. "Come on, girl," I said, but she ducked her head as I attempted to loop it around her neck. I finally got it on with a slipknot, but when I tried to lead her to the door, she dug in her heels and bleated at me. I dug in my own heels and started pulling. I'd almost gotten her to the door when she turned her head and slipped the rope, running back to the corner.

I was about to try again when there was yelling from outside. At the same time, there was a loud banging sound, and a cold wind slammed against the open barn door. I ran outside. As I turned to look at the fire, a cold, wet drop landed on my head. And then another. A moment later, the heavens opened and rain came sluicing down.

"Thank you," I murmured, looking up at the sky

with my hands open. As if in response, there was another series of bangs from the little house down by the creek. I glanced at it; the reflection of the flames danced in the windows, but when I turned to look at the fire, it was no longer marching up the pasture, and the wind had turned, pushing it away from the house and toward the dry creek.

"Perfect timing!" Tobias jogged over to me, hose still in hand, as I closed the barn door behind me.

"It's a miracle," I said. "I just hope it's enough." Tobias squeezed my arm; together, we hurried down to the firefighters.

"Will it put it out?" I asked Peter, who was still spraying down the area. I had to yell to be heard over the sound of the rain and the hose and the fire.

"No," he called back, "but between the rain and the changing wind, it should stop it long enough so that we can." He glanced over at me, his long hair slicked against his cheek. "Any water left in your stock tank?"

"There is," I said. "Use whatever you need. Can I help you out at all?"

"Probably best to steer clear and be ready to evacuate if things change. I've called for the second pumper truck."

I thanked him, but Tobias and I lingered a few minutes longer, surveying the damage. I'd lost about four peach trees, it looked like. Some of the trees down by the creek had been burned, too, which made me sad; I hoped the sycamore and cottonwood would bud out in the spring, but I didn't have high hopes. On the plus side, there was water in the creek now... which meant the fire's progress was blocked.

It was late by the time the fire was completely out. I ferried hot chocolate and coffee out to the two volunteer firefighters; it was the least I could do to thank them for coming out to save my farm.

When Peter and Ethan knocked on the front door of the farm, the rain was still coming down hard, pattering on the metal roof. "We got it," Peter said, "but we're drenched."

"Come in and warm up," I told them, taking off their jackets. "I'll get you some towels, and I have some leftover lasagna if you're hungry. I can't thank you enough for saving my home."

"Happy to do it," Peter told me. "And lasagna sounds terrific."

I threw a few more logs on the fire, heating up the kitchen, and grabbed fresh towels while Tobias and Quinn dished up some lasagna for Peter and Ethan. When we were all sitting around the table with mugs of chocolate, I turned to Peter. "I saw someone down by the creek when the fire started. Is there any way to tell if it might have been arson?"

Peter and Ethan exchanged glances. "We'll have to get an investigator out," Peter said.

"That's what I figured," I said.

"Who would have wanted to burn your place down?" he asked.

"Maybe it was Jed," Quinn said. "I came here last time... maybe he saw my truck and knew I was here."

"Or maybe it was someone who didn't want you looking in to what happened to Bug Wharton," Peter suggested. "I heard Serafine got out. I was thinking of stopping by to see her tomorrow."

I grimaced.

"What's wrong?"

"Tobias and I think someone tried to poison José down at the game ranch this morning," I said. "With Serafine out of jail, she could be a suspect again."

"Is he okay?"

"Tobias managed to get the poison out of his system."

"How?"

"Charcoal tablets and ipecac," I said. "The poison was in the Splenda in José's trailer, I think."

"That could have been anyone," Quinn said. "And if it was locked, it would have to be someone with a key."

"I have no idea if it was locked," I said. "People get a little lax about that here."

"But the Whartons had been in the city for years. Besides, everyone knows Serafine and the Whartons didn't get along. Wouldn't someone have noticed if she were there?"

"Good point," I said. "And why would she want to kill José?"

"Whoever tried to kill him must have thought he had some incriminating evidence," Tobias mused.

"Maybe we should head down to the hospital and ask him some questions," Quinn suggested.

"I get the feeling he wouldn't be too forthcoming," I replied. "He seemed kind of cagey about things."

"He did," Tobias agreed. "And Mitch Wharton didn't want us hanging around that trailer, either."

"I wonder what he was hiding."

Tobias ran a hand through his hair. "There are a lot of files in there. Maybe something attached to the ranch?"

"Or maybe the poisoned Splenda," I suggested.

"But why would Mitch kill his brother if he was the one who won the lottery?" Quinn asked. "He was the one with the money. It doesn't make sense. If anything, you'd think Bug would kill Mitch."

"Mitch won the lottery? I wondered how they bought the ranch," Peter said. "How much did Mitch win, anyway?"

I grabbed my computer and pulled it up. "Five million dollars."

"That'll pay for a few kangaroos," Tobias said.

"And a whole lot of acreage, apparently," Quinn said. "But you're right; it kind of knocks out the motive for Mitch."

"Here's an idea," I said. "What if whoever put the poison in the EpiPen poisoned the Splenda at the same time? So, there would be two ways to kill Bug... and because it was poison, you could be long gone when it happened."

"Or maybe lead investigators astray," Tobias suggested.

"It's a thought," I mused, "but it doesn't feel right. I think someone was trying to kill José because he knew something."

Tobias and I exchanged glances; I knew we were both thinking of Serafine's sister. Would hiding her relationship with Mitch be enough of a motive to kill him? Or was there something else going on?

"What about that lady in Houston?" Ethan suggested. "She could have planted the poison while she was here."

"I drove down to Houston to talk to her. She seemed surprised to find out Bug had died... but I wouldn't have pegged her as a murderer."

Tobias sighed. "Just because she didn't seem like a murderer doesn't mean she isn't one. There's got to be someone who had a reason to kill Bug and poison José."

"But who?"

"Maybe there's someone we don't know about," Tobias suggested. "Maybe someone who worked with both of them."

"Jed did," Quinn said slowly. "We all know he's as mean as a snake."

"He doesn't strike me as the poisoning type, though," Tobias said. "Besides, I don't know when he started working there. And I don't know what his motive would be."

"He hates authority." Quinn's chin jutted out. "I'll bet he reported to both Bug and José. In fact, I wouldn't be surprised if Mitch was next."

I glanced at Tobias. "I guess it's possible."

"What other options do we have?" he asked.

"Some folks might think it was me," Peter admitted. "After all, I organized the demonstration at the ranch. Plus, at the Witches' Ball, I wore that Grim Reaper outfit, and Aimee pulled that card..."

"Nonsense," Quinn said, glancing nervously at Peter. "Don't even talk about it. There's no way you were involved."

"We're coming up empty here," Tobias said. "Mitch was the one with the money, so he didn't have a motive; we're all confident Serafine didn't do it..."

"What would her motive be, anyway?" I asked.

"Anger over the way the animals are treated," Peter said. "And José was complicit in it. I can see how someone who was really passionate could see themselves as justified."

"I guess," I said, "but without a secondary reason, it feels weak." Tobias and I glanced at each other again, and I knew we were both wondering the same thing. Would protecting her sister really be enough to cause

Serafine to commit murder?

"It's always possible his Houston ex did everyone in," Quinn said, "and Lucy doesn't think she did."

"Someone probably lit that fire," Tobias pointed out. "You've been present both times, you're a former investigative reporter, and everyone knows you're trying to get Serafine off the hook."

"Are you saying someone was trying to scare me—or worse?"

"If you did see someone, and if whoever it was lit that fire, it's possible."

"Nothing like cozy, small-town life," I quipped.

"It was all pretty boring until you came around," Tobias said, grinning. "And it's not all been bad."

I gave Tobias a wry smile of my own. "Aww. You make me feel all warm and fuzzy inside."

He leaned over and kissed me on the top of the head.

"Hey there, you lovebirds. We have a serious situation here," Peter said.

I sighed. He was right, of course.

"Can you get someone to investigate the fire?" I asked him.

"I've already put a call in," he informed me.

I turned to Tobias. "I think we might want to make another trip to the ranch tomorrow, to check out those kangaroos again."

"Sounds like a plan," he said. "But in the meantime, I'm sleeping here tonight, in case someone decides to come back and finish the job."

"I'll stay, too, if that's okay," Peter said. "With the rain, though, it should be a little less dangerous."

"I'm not just worried about fire," Tobias said, glancing at the tranquilizer gun he'd left by the back door.

"I'm not, either," Peter said. "Unless you want to

come back to Green Haven with me?" he offered Quinn.

"If you think Jed knows you're here, it might not be a bad idea," Tobias suggested.

"I hate to desert you," Quinn said.

"I'll be with her," the handsome vet reassured her. "Does Jed know you and Peter are seeing each other?"

"He's moved back to Buttercup," Quinn reminded him. "He probably knows what I ate for breakfast."

"Good point," Tobias said.

"If you'd like, we can leave your truck here and you can go back with me," Peter said, looking at me. "As long as you don't mind, that is."

"Of course not," I told him. "I've got a man with a tranq gun handy. Speaking of which, how fast does that thing work?"

"It isn't immediate," Tobias said, "but I don't like carrying a gun with a bullet. We'll just have to lock up and take cover if need be. I'm a pretty good shot."

"Maybe I should learn," I said.

"It's worth knowing, but let's not worry about that tonight, shall we?" he said. "More hot chocolate, Lucy?"

"No, thanks," I told him. "I'm thinking a shower and then bed, to be honest. I smell like a smokehouse."

"I'm just glad you still have a house," Peter said. He hesitated. "I heard the ruckus at the old Ulrich house, by the way."

"It came when the storm came, didn't it?" I asked.

He nodded. "I'm not one to believe in ghosts, but..."

"Maybe it's a friendly, rain-bringing ghost," Quinn suggested. "Hey—you should check your well."

"Good idea!" I walked over to the kitchen sink and started the faucet. There was a popping sound as the air in the pipes passed through, then a brief spurt of water, then nothing.

"It may take some time for the water to filter down into the water table," Tobias pointed out as I turned off the faucet, disappointed. "Don't give up yet."

"It may be enough for bathing and drinking, but it's going to take a lot of rain to get to the point where I can use it for irrigation."

"Maybe we'll get more," he said. "If not, I'm sure we'll come up with a solution."

"Oh, I know there's a solution. It would help if I won the lottery. Think Mitch Wharton will share?"

"Good luck with that," Quinn said. "Anyway, I'm wiped."

"Me too," Peter said, standing up and stretching.

"I can't thank you enough for saving my home," I told Peter and Ethan.

"All in a day's work, ma'am," Peter said, tipping an imaginary hat. "Honestly, though, you got lucky... without that rain, I'm not sure we could have stopped it."

"Maybe, but the rain wouldn't have done it alone. Without you, the farm would be toast. Literally."

We made it to the next morning without any further disasters, thankfully. When the sun was up, Tobias and I took mugs of coffee and walked down to the burned area by the creek. My heart sank when I confirmed I'd lost four of my peach trees; their bark was blackened.

"You can replace them," Tobias reassured me as I fingered a dead branch.

"I know. It's just a little sad."

He gave me a hug, and together, we walked down

to the creek.

"I still can't think why someone would want to burn my house down," I said.

"The Jed theory is a possibility," he said.

"Why burn down my farm, then? Why not vandalize Quinn's cafe?"

"I agree; it's not a really strong possibility. The only other thing I can think of is that someone knows you're looking in to what happened to Bug Wharton, and wants you to keep out of it."

"I guess that's possible," I said as we reached the creek. "How do you look for signs of arson, anyway?"

"Well," he said, "in this case, there wasn't any lightning, you're not by a road, which means it didn't happen because someone threw a cigarette butt out a window, and as far as I know, there's not any electrical wiring down by the creek."

"All true," I confirmed. "Plus, I saw someone."

"You're sure you didn't get a look at the face?"

I shook my head. "Unfortunately not. What's this?" I stooped and pointed to a blackened piece of red plastic a few feet from the creek bed."

"It looks like the remains of a lighter," Tobias said, reaching for his phone to take a picture. "I'll tell Rooster; I know they're going to investigate, but this looks kind of like a smoking gun to me, so to speak."

"So, someone did try to set fire to my place."

"I'm just glad they didn't start with the house," Tobias said.

"I guess that's a silver lining of sorts," I said. But I still felt sick inside.

Chapter 18

THE HOSPITAL WAS A BIT of a drive from Buttercup; it was already ten by the time I pulled up in the visitors' lot. Tobias had helped me finish the morning chores before we parted ways. I had left the goats and the cows in the barn, just in case whatever had been snuffling around the night before decided to come back, before heading to visit José and drop by the Blue Onion to check in with Quinn.

"Be careful," Tobias had told me. "Let me know if you find anything out from José."

"I will. You too," I said. "And if you get a call out to the game ranch, let me know."

An older woman at the information desk gave me José Montoya's room number—he was in the Critical Care Unit—and I was glad to see Deputy Shames stationed outside.

"How's he doing?" I asked.

"He's coming in and out of consciousness," the deputy told me. "It looks like he's going to be okay."

"Was it poison?"

She nodded. "All the evidence went up in flames last night."

"What?"

"Someone torched the office at the ranch."

"You still have the samples you took, though, right?"

"We do have that," she said, looking over her shoulder. "Off the record, what Mr. Montoya drank was contaminated, so it was a good thing the sheriff took the samples. Because the rest of the physical evidence is gone."

I was right; someone had poisoned José. "Any working suspects?" I asked.

"Serafine Alexandre, of course. She was out on bail at the time it happened. If she didn't do it, it was bad luck."

"Or else someone planned it that way," I pointed out. "Someone set my place on fire last night, too."

"I heard there was a brush fire out on Dewberry Creek."

"We found a melted lighter down by the creek this morning," I said. "And I saw someone at the scene; I'm pretty sure it was arson."

"Maybe we've got a firebug."

"Or maybe someone's trying to cover their tracks," I said. "I visited Bug's ex-girlfriend in Houston... maybe someone doesn't want me poking around."

"When this guy wakes up, I'm hoping he can provide some answers."

"I'm glad you're guarding him," I said. "I was hoping to talk to him myself."

"I'll have to be in there with you," she told me.

"No problem Are you on the case?"

"A little bit," she said. "Why are you interested in it?"

"Because I think the sheriff arrested the wrong woman," I told her.

"It's not the first time," she replied.

"It certainly isn't," I told her as I walked into José's room.

The caretaker was hooked up to all kinds of wires,

and was disturbingly gray. As the machines beeped around him, I turned to the deputy. "Has family been in?"

"A woman was here last night, very upset. She went home, said she had to work, but asked me to take care of him and said she'd be back this morning."

"His wife?"

"I don't know. Her English wasn't very good, and my Spanish is terrible."

"Did she have any idea why anyone would want to poison him?"

"Not that I know of." She shook her head. "I'm sure they'll interview her—hopefully someone who speaks Spanish will be around to translate."

As she stood at the door, I sat down next to his bed.

"José?" I said in a gentle voice.

He moved his head back and forth, looking agitated.

"It's okay," I reassured him, touching his hand. He seemed to relax. "You're safe now. But I wanted to know if you had any idea who did this to you."

José started writhing a little bit. "Juego," he murmured.

"Juego?" I repeated.

"Juego," he said.

I turned to the deputy. She shrugged her shoulders. "He's been saying that on and off since he got here."

"Any idea what it means?"

She shook her head, looking like she was about to answer, when a woman burst into the room.

"He okay?" she asked, looking worried.

"He's fine," I said. She looked confused, and I gave her the thumbs-up. She relaxed and pulled up a chair across from José's bed, taking his hand and touching it tenderly. There was no wedding ring, but I got the impression they were a couple. Not for the first time, I wished I'd paid more attention in Spanish class.

As we sat there, he murmured "Juego" again. I looked at the woman, who was holding his hand. "Juego?" I asked.

"Juego." She said it crisply.

"Como se dice en inglés?" I asked, stretching the limit of my Spanish knowledge.

She pantomimed throwing something. I shook my head, and she repeated the word in Spanish.

"No comprendo," I said.

She sighed and tried again, this time miming pulling something down, but I wasn't understanding. "Good man," she said finally. "Help others. Why someone do this?" Her eyes filled with tears.

"I don't know," I told her honestly, repeating the word juego to myself. When I got home, I was going to have to look it up. I left a few minutes later, with assurances from Deputy Shames that someone who spoke Spanish would be in to interview the woman, and took her card so I could follow up.

"I'll make sure they look in to what happened at your place," she assured me.

"Thanks," I said. "And thanks for keeping an eye on José."

She nodded, and we shook hands again before parting ways.

"How'd your night go?" I asked Quinn when I walked into the Blue Onion an hour later.

"It was good," she said. "Any more issues at the farm?"

I shook my head. "I went to visit José, though."

"Is he doing okay?"

"Not great, but he's still kicking. He had a girlfriend or a wife there... she was very upset, but I don't speak Spanish and she doesn't speak much English, so we didn't really connect. He kept saying the word 'juego,' though. Any idea what that means?"

She shook her head. "I've got a Spanish-English dictionary upstairs, though. I'll go get it."

She hurried upstairs and came down a minute later, flipping through the pages. "It looks like it means 'game,'" she said.

"She looked like she was pantomiming throwing something..."

"Maybe dice? Like in Monopoly?"

"Maybe," I said, "but I got the feeling there was something else going on. I wish I knew what to do now," I said.

"I think we should talk to Serafine," Quinn said.

"Why?" I asked. "Neither of us think she's involved."

"No," Quinn said, "but I just have... I don't know. A feeling." She untied her apron. "There's not a lot of trade right now; why don't we head over there now? I'll ask Cindy to close up."

"You sure?"

"I am," she told me. "I'll just check in with her; she's at the cash register in the front." She disappeared to the front of the cafe and came back a moment later. "We're good to go," she told me. "Her sister Sophie will be here in fifteen minutes anyway; they can handle things together. I'll catch up on the baking later. Let's go!"

Both Aimee's Kia and Serafine's truck were parked outside the Honeyed Moon Mead winery when we pulled up a few minutes later.

"We'll get both of them," Quinn said as we got out of her truck and shut the doors.

Serafine met us at the front door of her little farmhouse. "Hey, y'all. Thanks for stopping by; I meant to say thank you for the mysteries."

"Anytime," I said. "How are you doing?"

She shrugged. "Okay, I guess. Why don't y'all come on in? I just brewed some mint tea."

"That sounds terrific," Quinn said as we followed her into the house. "Where's Aimee?"

"She's out tending the hives," Serafine said as she got out two more mugs and filled them with mint tea, then put a few chocolate chip cookies onto a plate. The kitchen was warm and cozy, with the woodstove burning in the corner and several Mason jars filled with dried herbs lined up on the counter.

"What are those for?" Quinn asked.

"I make teas with them, and incense," Serafine said. "And sometimes I use them for workings."

"Workings?"

"I guess you'd call them spells," she said.

"Really?"

"I told you I was a witch, didn't I?" she asked impishly.

"Please tell me you don't have eye of newt in one of those jars," Quinn said.

Serafine laughed. "No," she said. "Rose petals, some resins, sage... sage is wonderfully cleansing. In fact, I was going to use some for a working on clarity this evening."

"Clarity?"

"I wanted to ask the universe to uncover what happened to Bug Wharton," she told me.

"Speaking of Bug... I hate to ask this," I said as she put the plate on the table and handed me a mug, "but I hear you got out on bail yesterday."

"Yes," Serafine said, beaming. "That attorney you recommended is terrific."

I took a sip of tea. "This is delicious; what's in it?"

"Oh, mint and a few other herbs," she said. "I'll give you the recipe."

Quinn took a sip and groaned. "This is amazing. I'd love to serve this at the cafe."

"We might be able to work something out," Serafine said with a grin. "Now. Y'all didn't just come here for tea, did you?"

I shook my head and took another sip of the tea, which was mint laced with something earthy and sweet. "Did you hear about what happened to José Montoya?" I asked.

"No," she said. "Who is he?"

"He worked for Bug at the exotic game ranch. Someone poisoned him yesterday; I just got back from visiting him in the hospital."

"What?" She put down her mug. "There's something going on over there."

"That's what I think," I agreed. "I just don't know what."

"What brought you here?" Serafine asked again.

"I had a feeling," Quinn admitted. "I just felt like this was the right place to come."

Serafine nodded. "Maybe we should do the working now," she said. "But I think we should also consult the cards."

I shuddered, thinking of the death card Aimee had

pulled for Peter just before Bug died. "Have you talked with Aimee at all, by the way?"

Serafine shot me a knowing look. "We talked, yes. I know about what was going on with Mitch Wharton. I've known it for a while."

"She was afraid you'd be angry with her," I said.

"Not angry with her... worried for her, really. I didn't think it was a good choice for her. But I feel like we need to do a reading now. Hold on a moment; let me get my deck."

I reached for another chocolate chip cookie as she left the kitchen.

"I knew we were supposed to come here," Quinn whispered to me.

"You really think we're going to find out something from tarot cards?" I murmured back.

"Have an open mind," Quinn chided me. "You have any other ideas?"

She had a point, I thought as Serafine returned, unwrapping a deck of cards from a piece of turquoise silk.

"I'm going to have you ask the question," she said, handing me the cards. They were large, and there seemed to be an awful lot of them compared to a normal deck.

"Why me?"

"It feels right," she said. "Shuffle them as you ask your question, and hand them to me when you feel like you're done."

"What should I ask?"

"Whatever you want to know about what happened to Bug Wharton, is what I'd recommend. Follow your instincts."

"Okay." I shuffled the unwieldy cards and said, "Who

killed Bug Wharton?"

Serafine nodded as I handed her the deck, and I watched quietly as she laid out the cards and studied them.

"So, what do I do with this?" I asked when she put down the deck.

"There's a game of chance involved in this," she said, pointing to the card labeled wheel of fortune.

"Game," I said. "That's the word José said." I thought about what I'd seen in the trailer. "There were casino receipts there, at the ranch. Do you think that might be related?"

"Maybe. Also, Mitch Wharton won the lottery," Quinn pointed out. "Do you think that's it?"

"I have a sense that that's part of it," Serafine said, "but that there's more to it. Something more recent. And this woman is involved, too," she said, pointing a finger at the queen of cups. "Light hair, older."

"Evelyn?" I asked.

"Who's Evelyn?"

"Bug's ex-girlfriend," I said. "I talked to her in Houston."

"It might be worth it to talk to her again," Serafine said. "There is chance involved in this... games of chance. Games of chance gone wrong, and addiction, I think," she said, touching the devil card.

"Addiction? Like drugs or something?"

"Maybe," she said. "It's not completely clear... I think it's tied up with the games."

As she spoke, Aimee walked in. "Serafine, I..." She stopped short when she saw us. "Oh. What are you doing here?"

"We're doing a reading about what happened to Bug," Serafine said. "What do you make of the cards?"

Aimee walked over. "Deception, for sure," she said, pointing to a card labeled the five of swords. "Particularly with this card," she added, pointing to an eerie-looking moon card. "Who's this?" she asked, pointing to the queen of cups.

"I don't know," Serafine said. "Any ideas?"

"Bug's ex-girlfriend," Aimee said.

"That's what I thought," I agreed. "Does that mean she's involved?"

"Maybe... or she's relevant somehow."

"I haven't Googled her," I said.

"Maybe we should," Quinn said.

"I have my laptop over here," Serafine said. "I was doing some online PR... I'll grab it and we'll look her up. What's her name?" she asked as she put the laptop on the table next to the tarot cards. The combination of technology and magic made me grin: nothing like a little twenty-first century divination.

"Evelyn Crowley," I told her, and she typed it in.

"Does she live in Illinois?"

"No... Houston."

"Hmm. I'm getting a hit for an Evelyn Crowley in Peoria. Won the lottery two years ago."

"Wait... what?"

"It's right here," she said, turning the computer so I could see. "She won three million dollars in the Illinois lottery, two days before Christmas."

"Seriously?"

"Seriously."

"Didn't Mitch win the lottery, too?" Quinn asked.

"He did," I confirmed.

She Googled Mitch's name. "Sure enough. He won five million dollars on December 23 in Florida, three years ago."

"Wait... they both won the lottery, and on the same day?"

"Different states," Quinn pointed out.

"Still. There's coincidence, and then there's coincidence."

"You think it was rigged?" Serafine asked.

I pointed to the wheel of fortune card. "And José said something about games."

"Think he was talking about the lottery?"

"How would they be able to do that, though?" I asked.

"Maybe someone they knew worked for the lottery."

"Let's look," I said. We Googled Mitch and Evelyn, but no connections came up other than their win. "Besides," I said, "isn't it impossible to win the lottery if you work for the lottery?"

We were quiet for a minute. "Bug didn't win the lottery," Quinn said.

"But he's connected to both Mitch and Eva," I agreed. "Let's look him up. His real name is Jerome."

Serafine Googled his name, but the only thing that came up employment-wise was the company I'd brought up the other day. "He was with them for ten years," I said, "but I have no idea what they do. Google the name of the company and lottery," I suggested.

She did. "Nothing on the first few pages," she said, scrolling through. And then she stopped. "Wait," she said. "The Ohio Lottery Commission was a client of theirs."

"What did the company do for them?"

"Software," she said, and looked up at me. "Number generation."

"So, Bug fixed the lottery for them," I said.

"It's a good guess," Serafine said.

"But why kill him?" I asked. "It doesn't make sense."

"Maybe he was going to out them," Quinn suggested.

"But if he's the one who fixed it, wouldn't he be the one who would end up going to jail?" I asked. "We're missing something here." I looked back down at the cards. "Five of swords," I said, pointing at one of the cards. "What does that mean, again?"

"Deception. Something hidden," Serafine said.

"That could apply to the lottery scam, assuming that was what was going on," Quinn said.

"I think that's a pretty good assumption," I said. As I stared at the cards, I wondered what I was doing, taking my lead from a tarot card reading. On the other hand, it had been pretty helpful so far. "Here's the thing: Mitch and Evelyn profited from the lottery, but it looked like Bug was in charge of the ranch. Who owned the title?"

"We can check that, too," Serafine said. "I'll look up the address and run it through the appraisal district website." She typed for a moment, then clicked the mouse with a flourish and sat back. "Owner: Jerome Wharton. Appraised Value, $3,500,000."

"That's a lot of money," I said. "And I heard he paid in cash."

"Almost like he won the lottery," Quinn quipped. "Or some close friends shared their winnings."

"What do you think José knew?" I asked. "Obviously someone wanted to keep him quiet."

"Maybe he overheard something," Serafine suggested. "Or maybe he saw something." She did some more Googling.

"Whoever it was seemed to have some medical knowledge. Both times, the weapon was chemical."

"Evelyn was in medicine; I think she said she was a

nurse practitioner," I said.

"Really?" Serafine asked, and typed in her name. "You're right. She was in the oncology department at a hospital in Peoria."

I looked down at the cards. "Why would she want to kill him?"

"Maybe she ran out of money," Quinn suggested.

"Her house wasn't superposh," I agreed. "And she did have an argument with him that ended with a cattle prod to the family jewels."

"Think maybe she was in line to inherit something?" Serafine asked.

"I'll bet I can find out," I said.

"How?"

"I've got a friend in Houston who's good at ferreting that stuff out. Mind if I make a quick phone call?"

"Go for it," Serafine said. They waited as I made a quick call to an old reporter friend of mine. "She's going to see what she can find out," I told them when I hung up. "It might turn out to be a story for her, anyway; I don't feel so bad about asking."

"So, what do we do now?" Quinn asked.

"Whoever poisoned José must have had access to the trailer during the day before he died," I said. "Assuming it was the Splenda that did him in."

"Any word on that?"

"I'll check in again this afternoon," I told them. "I'd love to find a way to get back to the ranch to see if anyone remembers someone hanging around the trailer that afternoon."

"Jed's there," Quinn said in a tense voice.

"He is," I said. "So, I think you probably shouldn't join me."

"I don't want to go either," Serafine said. "I'm out on

bail, but I'm still a suspect."

"You might call Tobias," Quinn suggested.

"That's just what I was thinking," I said, and picked up my phone.

Chapter 19

"WHAT ARE WE LOOKING FOR again?" Tobias asked as we bumped up the driveway to the game ranch.

"Anything we can find," I said. "Someone set fire to my place to scare me off—I'm almost sure of it. I'm wondering if anyone saw Bug's ex-girlfriend around."

"So, you're thinking it's her?"

I told him what we'd discovered about the lottery that afternoon—and the fact that she'd worked as a nurse. I felt a little awkward talking about the cards, though, so I left that bit out. "If someone saw her around the ranch the night before José was poisoned, that'd be pretty close to a smoking gun."

"You went and visited her, too. Do you think she might have been the one to start your place on fire? To warn you off?"

"Or kill me," I added. "It's hard to know; I saw a face, but between the shadows and the heat distortion, I couldn't tell who it was. I don't even know if it was a man or a woman."

"Well, we'll see what we can find out," he said as he pulled up next to the burned husk of the trailer.

He parked the truck, and we both got out. "What are we officially here to do?" I asked as we ambled toward the kangaroo pen.

"Check in on the new arrivals," he said. "First, I think we need to talk to someone." A wiry man with dark hair and a plaid shirt was mucking out stalls in a building nearby. "I think we'll start there," he said.

"Hello!" he called in a cheery voice as he approached the worker.

The man ducked his head and continued to work. "We're here to look at the kangaroos," Tobias said.

The man gave him a blank look.

"Habla español?" Tobias asked.

The man smiled and nodded. "Sí."

My elementary Spanish wasn't enough to follow the conversation that sprang up between the men, but I did hear the word señora a couple of times. A few minutes later, Tobias nodded, looking satisfied, and put a hand on my elbow. "Let's go look at the kangaroos," he said, steering me away from the worker.

"What was that all about?" I asked.

"His name is Santos, and he's worked here since the ranch opened. Evelyn was here," he said. "The night before José died."

"Did he see her?"

"He said the señora—he didn't know her name—from Houston drove in. She and Mitch argued about something, and she peeled out."

"How does he know?"

"He was working late," Tobias said. "With Bug gone, it's been kind of chaotic."

"Does he know anything about José?"

"He didn't want to talk about him," Tobias told me. "I got the impression he was protecting him."

"If there was something in the trailer that would have incriminated José, maybe Santos burned it down to protect him."

"So, are you thinking a different person set the fire at Dewberry Farm?"

"It's possible," I said. "But why would he want to protect José?"

"Good question," Tobias said as we walked over to the kangaroos. "Maybe he was paying the help extra, or knew about something the workers were doing and let them off the hook."

"Like what?"

"José didn't want us hanging out around that barn." Tobias pointed to the small, ramshackle building about fifty feet from the kangaroo pen.

"Maybe we should check it out," I said. Together, we walked over to the weathered building. It had wood walls, a rusted metal roof, and no windows. Just a large barn door with a padlock. "What do you think it is?"

"Storage, would be my guess," he said. "Too bad it's locked." He grabbed the padlock and gave it a tug; to my surprise, it opened. "We're in luck; it isn't latched."

"Shall we?" I asked, and we stepped inside. When Tobias pulled the door shut behind us, it was as if someone had turned off the lights. Some narrow shafts of sunlight leaked through the boards on the walls, but it was very dark, particularly after the brightness outside, and there was a strong gamy smell. "I've got a flashlight on my phone," I said, flipping it on.

"Storage," Tobias confirmed as the beam swept over piles of boxes and old equipment to the right side of the door.

"Smells pretty bad for storage," I said. I swung the beam to the left and stifled a scream.

"What the..." Tobias trailed off.

"Is that a tiger?" I asked.

"It's not just one tiger," he said. "It's two. And a lion."

"They're in such small cages… and they're muzzled!"

"No wonder he didn't want us near this place,"Tobias said. "I'll bet these animals are here illegally."

"José knew about it, too," I told him. "Do you think that's why someone tried to kill him? They were afraid he was going to say something to someone?"

"It sure explains why someone might have burned down the trailer," Tobias said. "Records." He took a step toward the cages; one of the tigers let out a low growl as he approached. "Easy," he crooned in a sooth- ing voice. "Just taking a look. I won't hurt you."

"Are they sick?" I asked.

"A little malnourished, but they look okay."

"Why do they have them here?" I asked.

"Probably so people can hunt them," he said. "It's illegal. Some ranches hook hunters up with folks in Africa, but you can't legally do it here."

"No wonder José didn't want us in here," I said. "He didn't want us to find these guys. Maybe that's why someone tried to kill him."

"Because he was going to spread the word?"

As he spoke, a humming sound came from the cor- ner of the room. I flashed the light over to it; it was coming from one of two chest freezers.

"I'm kind of afraid to look in those," I said.

"I'll do it," he said. I trailed behind him, wincing as he opened it.

"What's in it?"

"Deer," he said.

"Exotic?"

"Nope. Local white-tailed," he told me. "They hav- en't really been processed."

"It's not deer season, though, is it?"

"Not until November," he said. "And these don't

look like they've been here for long. Someone poached them."

"Poor things," I murmured. "But why shoot and store deer when you've got exotics all over the place?"

Tobias looked over at the cages, and I shone my light on them. "They've got to eat," he said.

I shuddered. "There are two empty cages over there." I gestured to the corner were two were stacked on top of each other. "Do you think they had inhabitants?"

"Looks like it," he said, pointing to a tuft of orange fur in the cage.

"I don't want to think about where they are now."

He gave me a look. "I have an idea," he said.

"So do I," I said, running my light over the cats in the cages. "Let's get out of here."

"Good idea," he said. "I want to have a chat with Rooster about this. It's not illegal to have tigers as long as you have a permit, but it's illegal to hunt them."

"How do we prove it?"

"I don't know about that," he said. "But the ranch is supposed to have a permit for these animals, and I'm willing to bet they don't. And these conditions are just horrible for these poor animals."

"Let's get out of here," I said and took a step toward the door. Before we could get any farther, the door swung open.

Tobias and I shielded our eyes from the bright light as Jed surveyed us. "What are y'all doin' in here?"

"We were just leaving, actually," Tobias said.

"No," Jed said slowly. "I don't think you are." Before we could do anything else, he slammed the door shut. As Tobias and I sprinted toward it, we heard the snick of the padlock.

"Jed," Tobias called. "Let us out!"

No answer; he was gone.

"Crap," I said to Tobias. "What do we do now?"

"Find a way out of here was my first thought."

"I like the way you think. Any ideas on how?"

"No."

"Me neither," I said, pushing against the door. "For old wood, this is holding pretty well."

"Someone reinforced it recently," Tobias said, pointing to the fresh two-by-fours holding it together.

"Is there a hammer in here somewhere, or a crowbar? Maybe we can pull off those boards and weaken the door."

"Or go after the walls," Tobias suggested, pressing against a weak board.

I shone the light at the boards, then realized what I had in my hand. "You know, this flashlight doubles as a cell phone. Maybe I should use it."

"You call. I'll try to kick our way out of here."

As he kicked against the wall, I dialed Quinn. I was down to one bar on my phone; the reception was spotty at best. She wasn't answering; I left a quick message, then hung up and dialed Peter, and then Seraphine. Nobody picked up, so I left messages.

"Umm... have you considered 911?" Tobias suggested as he gave a board a swift kick that splintered it.

I dialed, and the dispatcher picked up.

"What is your emergency?"

"Someone locked us in a barn," I told her.

"What? I'm sorry, you're breaking up."

"A barn."

"A farm."

"No. A barn!" I said, slowly.

"A barn? Is there a window?"

"No," I said. "That's why I'm calling; we can't get

out. There are tigers in here, too."

"Fires?"

"Tigers!"

"Tigers?"

"Yes."

"Look. I don't have time for prank calls."

"This isn't a prank call."

She let out a weary sigh. "Fine. What's your location?"

"We're at the Safari Exotic Game Ranch."

"I'm sorry, ma'am, you're breaking up. Where?"

As I repeated what I'd told her, the phone beeped three times. The connection was lost.

"What happened?"

"The connection died," I said, just as there was a click and the barn door opened.

Chapter 20

IT WAS MITCH, WITH JED a few feet behind him. In his hand was a gun; I couldn't tell what kind, but it looked very businesslike. "What are y'all doin' in here?"

"We took a wrong turn," Tobias said. "And then your helper here," he added, jabbing a finger at Jed, "locked us in."

"Sorry about that," Mitch said, but made no move to unblock the doorway. "He was just following instructions."

"Why are there tigers in here?" Tobias asked. "They could probably use a little more room than they've got."

"It's legal to have tigers in Texas," Mitch said.

"If you have a permit for them," Tobias pointed out. "Plus, they need more space than these tiny cages."

"It's in process," Mitch told him.

"I'll be happy to check them out for you," the vet said, as if we were here on a routine visit and Mitch wasn't holding a gun. "I'll probably have to tranquilize them first, though."

"I don't remember calling for you to come out here today," Mitch said.

"I didn't get a chance to finish taking a look at the kangaroos," Tobias said smoothly, "so I decided to stop by. I'm sorry about José; you've had some bad luck here at the ranch lately, it seems."

"Yeah, well, you could say that. Now, why don't you tell me why you were really here in this barn?"

"I told you, we took a wrong turn," Tobias said.

"Forgive me if I don't believe you," Mitch said, and turned to look at me. "You've been hangin' around here a lot recently. I heard you went and paid a visit to a friend of mine in Houston, too."

"I thought she might be able to help figure out what happened to your brother," I said honestly. "Now, please let us get back to the truck. We've got things to do."

"I'm not sure that's such a good idea," he said. "Why don't you come with me?"

"I have things to do this afternoon," I said. "Thanks for unlocking the door. It never should have been locked in the first place." I stared hard at Jed.

"I don't think we're done here yet," he said.

"I think we are," Tobias replied.

"I don't know what you have in mind," I told him, "but people know we're here. If something happens to us, suspicion will fall on you."

"Maybe," he said. "Maybe not. Jed, get the keys from Dr. Brandt."

"No," Tobias said.

Mitch leveled the gun at him, then turned it to me. "You might want to rethink that. No one will think twice about a gunshot on the ranch. We've got a practice range not far from here."

Tobias hesitated, then dug in his pocket and handed over the key to Jed.

"Thank you, sir," Jed said in a sneering tone of voice, then turned to Mitch, Tobias's keys dangling from his hand. "Where do you want it?"

"Put it in the old barn on the south side," he said. "If there's a phone in the truck, turn it off and bring it to me."

"Yes, sir," Jed said, and hurried off toward the truck.

Mitch looked at the cell phone I was still holding in my hand. "I'll take that, thank you very much." Reluctantly, I gave it to him. In one smooth movement, he tossed it out into the dirt, took aim, and shot it. "Go pick it up," he ordered me. Feeling sick to my stomach, I retrieved what was left of my phone. The bullet had gone right through it, destroying the device. There was no way anyone was going to be able to track it.

"Now," he said, "I think it's time we got more comfortable." The rancher stared at me, the affable grin gone. There was something stony and scary in his eyes. "Ladies first," he said.

"If you don't let us leave soon, people are going to start asking questions about you," I pointed out.

"From what I hear, Rooster isn't the sharpest blade in the drawer when it comes to investigating. And to be honest, I think he'll thank me for getting rid of one more bee in his bonnet."

The mention of bees made me think of what had happened to Bug. "Did you put the bees in the truck?" I asked impulsively. If I could stall him long enough, maybe the police would get things worked out

"I did," he said. "The venom in the EpiPen was Evelyn's idea."

"That's right; she was a nurse. What I can't figure out is, what did you have to gain?" I thought for a moment about the piece of paper the bees had been wrapped in, and the brochures I'd seen in José's trailer.

"The ranch is mine now," he said.

"But you won the lottery."

"Only part of it," Mitch replied. "And I was getting down to the end of it. Bug was gettin' too big for his britches. I wanted to expand the business, but he tried to shut me down."

"You brought these tigers here for people to hunt, didn't you?" Tobias said.

"Smart vet," Mitch said. "It was a side hustle. Profitable, too."

"Bug didn't know about it?"

"We organized hunts while he was out of town. It was fine till he got sick and bailed on his California trip."

"So that's why you killed him," I said. "He was going to out you."

"We built this place together, and he was just goin' to shut me out. It wasn't right. Blood is thicker than water; that's the rule."

I didn't point out the fact that killing your brother wasn't exactly the friendly, familial thing to do.

"So, the deer were for the tigers?" Tobias asked.

Mitch nodded. "José shot white-tailed deer to feed 'em. Some went to the tigers, some went to some folks from Mexico he was helpin' out."

"José was getting cold feet, though, wasn't he? After Bug died?"

Mitch nodded. "Becomin' a liability."

"Did you help buy the ranch?" I asked.

Mitch shook his head. "Nah."

"But you won the lottery. And so did Evelyn."

"Bug got a big cut of that... and a few others, too. He was the big man on campus; the rest of us were just small fry."

"Still, you won quite a bit," I said. The more we knew, the more danger we were in, but the longer we stayed here, the higher the likelihood that Quinn or Peter would get the message and send someone out. "You got at least a million dollars, even if you split it, by my calculations. Where did all your money go?"

Mitch's lips formed a thin line. I thought of the casino brochure, and my conversation with Evelyn. "You gambled it all away, didn't you?" My mind turned to the wheel of fortune and devil cards. That was the addiction: gambling.

"Things between Bug and me weren't even. I was trying to level the playin' field. Had a run of bad luck."

"And so did Bug," Tobias pointed out.

"He deserved it. Lordin' it over all of us. Wouldn't lend us a dime."

"Why was Evelyn in town?" I asked.

"We were tryin' to talk him into one more windfall."

"The lottery scam," I said. "The December 23 winnings. He knew what the numbers would be that day, didn't he?"

"It was a code he slipped in. He needed us to collect, though. If he'd won it himself, it would have been obvious."

"So, you did it in different states, in different years. How much did he take?"

"Half each time," Mitch said. "And we weren't the only two, either. No, Bug's been collectin' for years. Only once he was happy, he quit and left us hangin'."

"And when you were in trouble, he wouldn't help you out."

"Not just that. He kept me from doin' what I needed to to pay up!"

"You had debts," I said quietly. "Gambling debts. That Coushatta place isn't just a resort," I realized, thinking of the credit-card statement I'd seen in the trailer. "It's a casino."

"It is a casino," he admitted. "But I'm not in debt any-more. Once that will is probated, I'll be sittin' pretty."

"It all comes to you?"

He nodded. "I'll give some to Evelyn of course." I wasn't putting any money on that; I was guessing she was slated for extermination, too.

"Why'd she go after Bug?" I asked.

"He wouldn't help her out," he said. "She'd fallen on hard times. He told her she'd had her chance. That's what... inspired her to help me come up with a plan to take care of him."

"What are you going to do about José? He survived."

"I'll go see him," he said. "Finish what I started. Besides, odds are they can't prove anything once the cats are gone. I'll just remind him what might happen if he decided to tell tales. I know about his poachin'."

"Did you set fire to my property?"

"That wasn't me, but I heard about it," he said. "Someone else must not like you."

"What about the trailer?" Tobias asked.

"That was me, I confess. Less obvious than breakin' into it. Nothin' in there was crucial to the business anyway."

"Where are the other two tigers?" Tobias asked, seemingly out of the blue.

"We had a hunt," Mitch said. "Two weeks ago."

Tobias sighed. "Were they killed?"

"One of them was," he admitted.

"Where's the other one?" I asked.

"Could be anywhere. Fence was down. Haven't seen it on the property."

"Wait a minute," Tobias said. "There's a full-grown tiger loose in Buttercup?"

"Is that what we saw by the barn the other night?" I asked, shivering.

Tobias turned to me. "I don't know, but I'll bet that's what did in the oryx."

"But that was after the fences got fixed," I said.

Tobias shook his head. "Tigers can climb, you know. Tall fences won't stop them."

"Thanks for the info, professor," Mitch sneered. "Don't you think I figured that out?"

"Well, what are you going to do about it?" Tobias asked.

"No one knows we have tigers here. Except you."

"And the people who paid to hunt them," I pointed out.

"They're not too likely to go to the authorities, are they?" Mitch asked. "Besides, now that the place is mine, I can wind that down. Get rid of the remaining cats."

"What are you going to do with them?"

"There's a market for them," he said, looking very satisfied with himself. "I've got two buyers in Louisiana, coming to pick 'em up tonight. But enough talk. Let's go."

He marched us out of the barn at gunpoint.

"Where are we going?"

"You'll find out," he said, tossing me a key and pointing us in the direction of his truck. "Get in. You drive," he told me. "I'll hold the gun."

I climbed into the driver's seat with Tobias beside me. He reached out to squeeze my hand as Mitch slid into the seat behind me. "I'm pointing it at your boyfriend," he told me. "So don't get any ideas about heroics."

I followed Mitch's directions down a dirt road track, then off to a barely visible rutted roadway that wound through trees and ended at a dilapidated barn. The doors were open; I could see Tobias's truck inside.

"Stop here," he told me, and I parked the truck. "Get out," he said. Adrenaline pulsed through me. I looked over at Tobias; he squeezed my hand again. "Stop lollygaggin'," he said.

I felt like I was moving in slow motion as I got out of the truck. Was this how things were going to end for Tobias and me? In an old barn on the Safari Exotic Game Ranch?

"Are you going to poison us, too?" I asked.

"No," he said. "You're going to have a lovers' quarrel. It'll be a murder-suicide."

"Everyone knows we wouldn't do that," I said. "They'll find out it was you."

"They haven't so far," he said. "That witch is on the hook for everything."

"You really don't like Serafine, do you?" I asked as we stood together outside the barn. Mitch was leveling the gun at Tobias while Jed stood in the background.

"She was tryin' to keep Aimee from seein' me. Got her way, too. She deserves it."

"You really think Aimee is going to want to see you just because her sister went to jail?"

"Now that I have the means to help bankroll her business, why wouldn't she?"

"Because you're a murderer, maybe?" Tobias suggested.

"She doesn't know that," Mitch said. "Besides, it's what you do when you really love someone. If it weren't for Aimee, I never would have gotten into the gambling in the first place, so she's as guilty as I am."

Tobias and I exchanged glances. Mitch Wharton had either gone to graduate school for a PhD in rationalization or he was seriously unhinged. I was guessing the latter.

"Get in the truck," he ordered us.

"My truck?" Tobias asked. Tobias's truck was parked inside the barn; there was no sign of Jed, though.

"Your truck," he confirmed. "We're all going to go for a ride."

So, it wouldn't be at the exotic game ranch after all. It made sense; he'd want to keep himself clear of everything. What would he do about Jed?

Tobias climbed into the driver's seat. I slowly moved around the truck, Mitch's gun pointed at my head, and got into the passenger side, my mind racing as I tried to figure out how to get out of this awful situation. As I closed the door to the truck, Mitch reached for the back door. At that moment, there was a low, terrible growl. My insides turned to water. Mitch yanked at the door, dropping the barrel of the gun for a moment.

"Duck!" Tobias said. I didn't hesitate. As I hurled myself to the floor of the truck, Mitch yelled. There was a clatter, then a horrible scream.

"The tiger's got him!" Tobias said. Without hesitation, he yanked at the door handle and kicked the driver's side door open.

"What are you doing? No!" I yelled. As I watched, he sprinted to the back of the truck and grabbed the tranq gun from the rack in the back. I looked out the window to where Mitch lay on the ground, writhing; the gun he'd been holding was nowhere to be seen, and the tiger was mauling his leg. The rancher was screaming like I'd never heard anyone scream before.

I looked back at Tobias. He took aim, cocked the tranquilizer gun, and fired. The tiger let out an angry yowl and dropped Mitch's leg, then turned its eyes on Tobias. The dart protruded from its left shoulder. I prayed it would work fast—and be enough to fell the cat.

Unfortunately, it wasn't working fast enough. Tobias shot a second time, landing a second dart next to the first as the tiger advanced. I watched the muscles bunch in its haunches; it was preparing to pounce.

Adrenaline pumped through me. I propelled myself up and over the seat, then grabbed the handle of the back door. As the tiger launched itself, I threw open the back door.

The big cat hit the door with such force, it jarred my whole body. "Run!" I yelled to Tobias. But he ignored me. As I watched, he quickly reloaded, then lifted the gun another time and loosed a third dart. Then, as the tiger staggered to its feet and I struggled to close the truck's back door, he rounded the truck and yanked open the door to the driver's seat. He turned the key in the ignition and gunned the engine. A moment later, the truck burst out of the barn, the side mirror thwacking against the wood frame of the door as we left the tiger and its former keeper behind us.

Chapter 21

A S TOBIAS RACED DOWN THE dirt track toward the main buildings, I held the bent door shut from the backseat. "How long until the tranquilizer gun takes effect?"

"I don't know," he told me. "I'm hoping only a couple of minutes. I hit the cat three times; hopefully that will speed it up, but not kill it."

"A tiger can do a lot of damage in a couple of minutes, I imagine."

"I know," he said, grimacing. "I didn't really have much of a choice, though."

"Mitch Wharton isn't facing particularly good odds at the moment," I observed.

"No," Tobias said shortly, taking a hard turn in the road. A moment later, we were at the main compound, where two police cars were waiting for us. Serafine was there, too, hugging herself, her eyes dark with worry. It looked like at least someone got the message.

"What's going on here?" Rooster asked as Tobias screeched to a halt and I practically tumbled out of the backseat of the truck. "I heard y'all were in trouble, but you look okay to me."

"Mitch Wharton tried to kill us, but was attacked by a tiger," I told the sheriff. "Tobias hit the tiger with three tranquilizer darts, but he doesn't know how long they'll take to work."

"Jed Stadtler's back there somewhere, too. We need to go immobilize the tiger and save Mitch."

"Tiger on the loose? I heard about chupacabras, but..."

"We've got to hurry," I said. "Mitch is in terrible danger."

"I've got just the thing for that," Rooster said, reaching for his sidearm.

"No," Tobias said. "I don't want to kill it."

"What exactly do you propose we do, then?"

"I don't know," he said, "but call an ambulance and follow me."

"But..."

Neither of us waited for an answer. We got back into the truck—I stayed in the back so I could keep the door shut—and Tobias put it in reverse, then peeled out, going back the way we came.

"Think they'll follow?" I asked.

Tobias glanced in the rearview mirror and I looked behind. Rooster was clambering into his car. "Yup."

"Slow down or they'll lose us," I said.

"We don't have much time," Tobias reminded me.

"I don't want to get there alone, do you?"

"Good point." He paused until Rooster was mobile, then gunned the engine again. All too soon—but maybe not soon enough—we rounded a bend and arrived at the old barn.

Things looked very different from the way they had a few minutes earlier. Both the tiger and Mitch were passed out on the dirt floor of the barn... and Jed Stadtler was standing over them both, holding the gun Mitch had dropped.

"Uh-oh," I said.

"Good thing we have Rooster," Tobias said.

"Is that a joke?" I asked as the two cop cars pulled in behind us. Jed's eyes widened, but he didn't drop the gun.

"What's goin' on here?" Rooster asked as he clambered out of the front seat of the cruiser.

"I don't know," Jed lied.

"Yes, you do," Tobias said curtly, "but I don't have time for you now."

"Careful," I warned him as he slipped out of the truck and approached the unconscious tiger—and Mitch.

"Don't shoot me," Tobias advised Jed as he squatted next to Mitch and put a finger on his neck. "He's alive, but bleeding badly," the vet said. He unbuttoned his shirt and yanked it off, then fashioned a tourniquet around his leg. "We need an ambulance." He turned to the passed-out tiger. "And we need to get this cat immobilized."

"Do we take it to the cage, or bring the cage here?" I asked.

"Immobilize the tiger first," he said. "I've got some rope in the back of the truck I use for livestock; we can make it work, I think. I need to check its vitals, too; I hit it with a lot of sedative."

"I'll get the rope," I said as Tobias squatted by the big cat.

"Looks like you hit Mitch with a lot, too," Rooster commented from a safe distance.

"Well, based on what his leg looks like, he may thank me," Tobias pointed out. I grabbed a coil of rope from the bed of the truck and hurried over to Tobias.

"I've never tied up a tiger before," he said.

"How different from a cow can it be?" I asked. He gave me a look. "I have faith in you," I assured him.

"That's so encouraging," he said with a grin as he expertly tied the tiger's paws together—kind of a big-cat hog-tying approach—and then plucked the two darts from the cat's shoulder.

"How long will it last?" Rooster asked as the ambulance pulled up outside the barn. Two paramedics came hustling out, then stopped when they saw the tiger.

"I've got it under control," Tobias said authoritatively. I hoped he was right.

"What do we do now?" I asked.

"Get the cage," he said. "I think it's safer than moving the tiger. Can you handle it?"

"I'll go with her," Deputy Shames volunteered. I smiled; in all the excitement, I hadn't noticed her.

"Take the truck," Tobias advised. "You can fit it in the truck bed."

"Will do," I said as he tossed me the keys.

A half hour later, the tiger was safely in the cage in the back of the truck, Rooster was trying to figure out who he should call about the tigers locked in the barn, and Mitch was headed to the hospital under guard. Jed had tried to tell an alternate story about what had happened, but nobody was buying it; even Rooster didn't trust him.

"You're not supposed to have a firearm in your hand when you're on parole," he told Jed. "You're comin' in with me."

For the first time ever, I found myself agreeing with something Rooster had said.

Chapter 22

HALLOWEEN DAWNED COLD AND CLEAR, a mix of freshness and smoke in the air as I finished my chores. To celebrate Serafine being cleared—and Jed winding up back in jail—I'd invited my friends to a Halloween potluck celebration at the farm. The Kramers couldn't make it—they were busy with school events—but Peter, Quinn, Serafine, Aimee, and Tobias had RSVPed yes. I busied myself taking care of things around the house and made a quick trip to the Red and White Grocery. The front of the store was decked out with beautiful golden chrysanthemums and a small pile of pumpkins; inside was a hard-to-pass-up bin loaded with half-price candy for trick-or-treaters. I was checking out with three bags of Snickers and a bag of tortillas when Maria walked in the door, wearing a black sweater with a bright orange jack-o'-lantern sewed onto it.

"Lucy!" she said. "I heard you had a bit of excitement."

"You could say that. You're looking festive today."

"Thanks! I love holidays," she said. "But enough about that. Murderers on the loose, tigers prowling in Buttercup... what is this world coming to?" she asked. "Everyone said it was a chupacabra, but I knew it couldn't be. I'm just glad we're safe."

"Me too," I said. "Although something was outside my barn the other night, and it didn't look like a tiger. It looked almost wolflike."

"Ed Chovanek trapped a mangy German shepherd last night and a lot of us have been wondering if that's what's been hanging around. It's bony as all get-out, but it's huge."

"What did he do with it?"

"Took it to Tobias for treatment this morning," she said. "I think he's hoping Serafine will help him get it well and adopt it out; it's such a relief that Rooster finally figured out what happened to those poor men."

I decided not to comment on Rooster's investigative abilities. "Any word on José?" I asked, considering Maria seemed to know everything.

"Oh, he's coming around," she said. "He confirmed what Rooster suspected," she said. "Mitch Wharton's in jail for murder; apparently, he ran up hundreds of thousands of dollars in debts gambling and killed his brother to pay them off. Word is Bug's ex was involved, too... Can you believe Bug rigged the lottery? Sounds like he deserved what he got."

I wasn't sure anyone deserved to be murdered, but I kept my thoughts to myself.

Edna Orzak, who was all ears, helped me bag my groceries as Maria spoke. Which meant the news would be all over Buttercup by the end of the day—if it wasn't already. "I heard you found a diary or somethin' in that haunted house you moved over to Dewberry Farm," she said as she put the second pack of fun-sized Snickers bars into my bag. "Ever find out anything about the ghost?"

Maria's smile drooped a bit. "I translated the diary, and it was interesting—all about life in that time, and

Indian raids, and crop failures... but nothing about what happened to her."

"When did the diary end?" I asked.

"A few days before Ilse disappeared," Maria sighed. "I know what the cameo is from, though; it was from her aunt in New York. There was a lot of talk of correspondence between them, but she must have put the letters somewhere else. She sent it to Ilse for her sixteenth birthday."

"So, we may never know what happened," I said, still thinking of the rusty knife that had been hidden with the diary and the cameo.

"No," Maria said, "but there were a lot of Indian raids at that time."

"Maybe the house was built on an Indian graveyard, and they came for retribution!" Edna suggested, eyes wide. "So you have double ghosts in the house... the Indians and the girl they killed!"

Maria and I exchanged glances. "Maybe," I said. "We may never know, unfortunately."

"I should be glad to have a record from my ancestors," Maria said, "but I have to say I was hoping for a bit more closure."

"Maybe we'll turn up something else during the renovation."

"Maybe," Maria replied, not sounding hopeful. "At any rate, I've got to go; I'm supposed to make a Jell-O brain mold for a Halloween party tonight, and I need some evaporated milk to make it gray."

"Ugh," I said. "Enjoy!"

"I'll try." She grinned, adjusting the hem of her Halloween sweater. "Oh—by the way —the German Club voted to donate ten thousand dollars to the renovation... all we ask is that you preserve the outside and the beautiful stenciling downstairs."

"Really?" I asked.

"And Jacob Mueller has agreed to help out at a discounted rate; he's kin, too, you know. In fact, I was looking at ancestry.com the other day, and I think I found a Vogel connection, too. Your grandmother and my grandmother were first cousins!"

"So maybe the house was meant to be at Dewberry Farm after all." I felt the rightness of it as I said it.

"Feels like it," she said. "Anyhow, we'll figure out the details later this week. Happy Halloween... and do let me know if you find out anything else while you're renovating."

"Thanks, Maria!" I called as she headed back toward the canned milk.

"Sounds more like Christmas than Halloween to me," Edna said with a twinkle in her eye.

"You're telling me," I said, ripping open one of the bags of Snickers and offering her a fun-sized bar. "Happy Halloween," I told her.

Her face lit up. "Thanks!"

"My pleasure," I answered through a fun-sized bar of my own.

Tobias came early to help me prepare. As we set to work in the kitchen, Chuck dogging our heels and hoping for stray scraps, I filled him in on what Maria had told me, and he told me about the German shepherd he'd treated that morning.

"Do you really think he was what we saw the other night?" I asked as I checked on the chicken I'd put in the oven to bake.

"Maybe," he said. "He's malnourished and has a terrible case of Demodex, but he's a good dog. I think with the proper treatment, he'll make someone a loyal companion."

"What's Demodex?"

"A type of mange caused by mites. It's treatable, but it's a long process."

"I heard Serafine offered to help out."

"She did," he said. "She's got some extra room; plus, she's already treating Chiquis for Demodex, so she knows what she's doing. I'll donate the medical care and supplies."

"That's lovely of you," I said.

"It's the least I can do," he said. "I wish it were as easy for the tigers."

"No luck?"

"I'm working with a few organizations on getting them back to health and rehabilitated, but apparently there are a lot of homeless tigers in Texas at the moment. I'm hoping we can find a zoo or sanctuary that will take them."

"There's a big homeless tiger population here? Why?"

"People buy them as pets when they're little, and then they grow up."

I shook my head. "I don't understand people."

"That makes two of us," he agreed, giving me a hug. "But all we can do is try to do some good and look out for people who need help. Like you did, with Serafine."

"And you're doing with that poor dog," I said. "And those tigers."

He kissed my head. "Every little bit counts. I'm glad you're in my life."

"I'm glad you're in mine," I replied, and I must confess the kitchen work took a bit of a backseat for a while.

We were shredding chicken for enchiladas when Serafine pulled up outside with a blue bag slung over her shoulder and a wine carrier in her hand, containing what looked to be several bottles of mead and some spices.

"You're here early," I said as she walked in and set the carrier down on the counter.

"I promised I'd dowse the place for you," she said.

"Is Aimee coming later?"

She grimaced. "I couldn't get her to come. She's still upset about everything that went on. It'll take time."

"I'm sorry," I said.

She shrugged. "Life has its ups and downs; I'll help her through it as best I can. You have a few minutes to dowse? I'll get the mead warming when we get back."

"I'll finish the chicken," Tobias told me. "You go on out."

"Thanks," I said.

As I followed Serafine outside, she opened the voluminous blue bag she had brought. "I brought my sticks."

"Those look like bent coat hangers," I said.

"That's exactly what they are." She beamed. "Ready?"

"Why not?" I asked, thinking you got what you paid for. And if nothing else, I'd get to spend a few minutes with Serafine.

"Good luck," Tobias said with a wink and a grin. "If I see a geyser, I'll know you were successful."

I stuck my tongue out at him and followed Serafine

out the door.

"How's Aimee really holding up?" I asked.

"She's not great, but I think she's going to be all right," Serafine said. "I think she's still a little hung up on Mitch, to be honest, even with everything he did. There's something about someone wanting you so much they're willing to commit murder to have you."

"Sounds kind of icky to me," I said.

"Me too," Serafine said. "She must have some karmic stuff she's working through. I'll see if I can do a clearing ritual when I get home... I can't thank you enough for finding out the truth about what happened to Bug and José. Without you, I'd likely be spending this Halloween—and many more—in jail for something I didn't do."

"Thank you so much for getting the police out there," I said. "You were a lifesaver. Literally."

"Of course," she said. "Any idea what's going to happen to the tigers?"

"They're going to be rehabilitated, but after that, we're not quite sure yet. Tobias is working with a few places; he'll be sure to get them placed. At least we now know what the chupacabra was."

"A neglected German shepherd... poor thing. He's super-sweet; I'm thinking of calling him Chupa."

"I like it!" I told her.

"Now," she continued, holding the bent hangers out in front of her as if they were antennae. "Ready?"

"You're in charge," I said. "What do they do when they find water?"

"You'll see," she said. "Where's the original well?"

"Over there," I said, pointing to the well house, which was on a knoll not far from the house.

"Hmm. Let's head down to the creek. Easier to get

to the water table there, maybe."

"Here's hoping," I said. Together, we walked down to the creek, Serafine holding her hangers out in front of her, me following her like an attendant. "They're just swinging."

"You'll see," she repeated with a grin.

We took several trips back and forth across the field and the burned stubble. The hangers wobbled, and occasionally swayed a little bit, but on our sixth pass up from the creek, in part of the burned field, two things happened at once: the rock moved under Serafine's foot, and the two hangers swung toward each other, then far apart.

"Whoa," Serafine said, squatting down. "What's this?" We smoothed the dead foliage away to reveal a large, flat slab of limestone.

"What's this doing here?"

"I think there may be something underneath it," she said. "Help me out?"

Together, we grabbed one edge of the slab and pulled. The stone moved a few inches, enough to reveal a dark cavity lined with roots. The edges were lined with stones—stones that someone had laid, based on the evenness with which they'd been placed. Serafine stood up and held out the hangers. They swung together, then apart. She then squatted down and grabbed a small pebble from near the opening, dropping it in. After a short moment, it made a satisfying plunk.

"I don't think you're going to have to drill a new well after all, Lucy. You already have one."

Peter and Quinn arrived as we hurried back to the house.

"We found a well!" I announced.

"You're kidding me! Where?" Quinn asked.

"In the burned area," I told him. "I don't know how deep it is, but I'm hoping it'll be enough!"

"Let's get Tobias and take a look," Peter suggested.

We all hurried over to the slab Serafine and I had found. As we tramped around the area, we confirmed that I not only had a well, but likely the ruins of an older structure nearby. Now that the fire had gone through, Peter, Quinn, and Tobias were able to find the remains of a foundation and possibly a cistern belonging to a much older building.

"You'll need to install a pump and a new line, but this may be the answer to your water troubles," Peter said when he'd finished inspecting the area. "I hope it's deep!"

"We'll find out," I said. "In the meantime, we should probably cover it up again, don't you think?"

We slid the slab back over the old well and turned back toward the farmhouse, whose windows glowed yellow in the darkening evening.

"There's history here you don't know about, my dear," Tobias said, kissing me on the head as we walked back to the house. The sun had sunk below the horizon, and a full moon hung in the sky, silhouetted behind blackened tree branches where the fire had torn through.

My eyes drifted to the silent, empty house I'd moved to the property. "Lots of history," I echoed. "Including what happened in that house; Maria came up empty on the diary."

Quinn slapped her thigh. "I almost forgot to tell you!

I know what's making the banging noise."

"What?"

"I talked with Maria's cousin—he told me he's going to be doing some renovations on the house—and he heard it, too, when he was checking it out a few weeks ago."

"So, he heard the banging?"

"He did," she confirmed. "What we thought was a ghost? It was just the old metal in the roof contracting when the temperature dropped. It happens a lot in these old houses, apparently."

"Hmmm," I said.

Serafine looked doubtful, too. "Can we walk over? I'd love to see it."

"Sure," I said, shivering. Dinner was in the oven, so we had some time, but the full moon and the darkness blanketing the abandoned house gave me the heebie-jeebies. "This place creeps me out at night," I confessed.

"It has a sad feeling, I'll give you that," Serafine said as we approached. "But not evil."

"Can you tell what happened here?"

She stepped up onto the porch. "She fled," she said in a voice of wonder. "Had to leave everything behind."

"What?"

"There was a raid... she ran. She was planning on leaving anyway, but she didn't have time to pack. She grabbed money out of her parents' room and ran into the woods."

"Where did she go?"

"She went north," Serafine told me. "Another family member was there... she sent a letter to her parents when she arrived. They never got it. They're all still here, trying to communicate with one another."

"Their ghosts?"

"Their spirits," she corrected me. "There's a veil between them."

"So, the house is haunted," Quinn said.

As if in reply, there was a bang from upstairs.

"It is," Serafine said. "Hold on. It's good we're here tonight; the veil is thinnest."

"What about the knife?"

Serafine closed her eyes. "It was to be protection," she said. "It wasn't blood, she's saying. Just rust. She never used it. She still feels bad... says you'll find her in the records of New York City. She says to tell Maria."

Quinn and I exchanged looks in the light of the rising moon.

"Can you help them communicate?" I asked.

"I think so," she said. We were all quiet for several minutes. I could feel something from the house; something that made my skin prickle. Serafine murmured a few things in what sounded like French, made a few signs with her hand, and then rummaged in her blue bag again. A flame flared in the darkness.

"What's that?"

"Sage," she said. "It's done; the parents have peace, and they are willing to depart. Now, I want to smudge the place."

"It's not safe upstairs," Tobias warned her as she stepped up on the porch.

"The smoke will rise," she replied placidly, a small smile on her lips.

"Need company?" I asked.

"No," she said. "They asked me to come alone."

As we all watched, she stepped into the house, using the lighter as a candle. We tracked her progress from room to room by the glow in the windows; when she appeared at the door, I had to confess the house felt lighter. "All done," she said. "They might come back and visit from time to time, but they are free now."

"Thank you," I said.

"It does feel different," Quinn said slowly.

My phone beeped as we stood there.

"I think the casserole's done," I said. "We should head up. Anything else we need to do here?"

"No," Serafine said with a smile as we headed back up to the farmhouse. "Everyone here is at peace."

"I'm so relieved," I said. "Where did you learn to do all that?"

"I'm a fifth-generation voodoo priestess on my mother's side, and my paternal grandmother was a witch. I'm twice-blessed; I grew up with all this," she said.

"It must be so weird walking through the world and seeing and knowing all this... stuff."

"It adds depth," she said, "but it can be a challenge some days." Her smile curved into a grin. "But this evening, I confirmed what I've always thought; there's someone here watching out for you, Lucy Resnick."

Goose bumps broke out on my arms and legs. "Grandma Vogel?"

Serafine nodded. "She says hello. She's delighted you're at the farm."

"She's not... trapped here, is she?"

"No, not at all. She's here because she wants to be; she can go at any time."

"That's a relief."

"Wait... there's one more thing."

"What?" I asked breathlessly.

Serafine's eyes were misty, as if she could see something the rest of us couldn't. "Got it," she said.

"What?"

"She told me to ask when you're going to make snickerdoodles."

I blinked at Serafine for a moment. Then I laughed; snickerdoodles had always been her favorite. "Tell her I'll make them tomorrow, just for her. And that I love her."

"She knows that already," Serafine said with a smile, and linked her arm in mine as we all headed back to my grandmother's cozy farmhouse.

MORE BOOKS BY KAREN MACINERNEY

To download a free book and receive members-only outtakes, short stories, recipes, and updates, join Karen's Reader's Circle at www.karenmacinerney.com! You can also join her on Facebook at facebook.com/AuthorKarenMacInerney and facebook.com/karen-macinerney.

The Dewberry Farm Mysteries
Killer Jam
Fatal Frost
Deadly Brew
Book 4, Title Forthcoming (Fall 2018)

The Gray Whale Inn Mysteries
Murder on the Rocks
Dead and Berried
Murder Most Maine
Berried to the Hilt
Brush With Death
Death Runs Adrift
Whale of a Crime
Claws for Alarm (Spring 2018)
Cookbook: The Gray Whale Inn Kitchen
Blueberry Blues (A Gray Whale Inn Short Story)
Pumpkin Pied (A Gray Whale Inn Short Story)

The Margie Peterson Mysteries
Mother's Day Out
Mother Knows Best
Mother's Little Helper

Tales of an Urban Werewolf
Howling at the Moon
On the Prowl
Leader of the Pack

RECIPES

MULLED HONEY WINE

2 cinnamon sticks
5 whole allspice
5 black peppercorns
5 cardamom seeds
7 whole cloves
3 one-inch pieces of candied or fresh ginger
1 orange, sliced
2 liters mead (I like Blessed Bee)
Honey to taste
Amaretto (optional, but recommended)
6 inch square of cheesecloth
Kitchen twine

Wrap the spices in a piece of cheesecloth and secure it with twine to make a spice bag. Combine the mead, the spice bag, and the orange slices in a pot and bring to a boil, then reduce heat to a simmer. Let the mead and spices simmer for at least 30 minutes, then discard the orange and spice bag and add honey to taste.

Serve hot in a glass (with an optional shot of amaretto). If desired, garnish with an orange twist or a cinnamon stick.

HALLOWEEN PUMPKIN BARS

Cake:

Preheat oven to 350 degrees. Cream butter and brown sugar until fluffy, then beat in eggs. Add 1 teaspoon vanilla extract and beat until smooth, then beat in baking soda, baking powder, salt, cinnamon, ginger, and nutmeg. Mix in flour alternately with pumpkin. Do not overmix. Spread in buttered and floured 9" x 13" baking pan and bake for 20-25 minutes.

Cream cheese frosting:

Beat cream cheese and butter until fluffy, then add confectioners sugar , 1 teaspoon vanilla extract, and 1/2 tsp almond extract. Beat until smooth. Frost cooled pumpkin bars.

LUCY'S APPLE DUMPLINGS

Unbaked pastry for double-crust pie (use frozen from the store or your favorite recipe)

> *6 large Granny Smith apples, peeled and cored*
> *½ cup butter*
> *¾ cup brown sugar*
> *1 teaspoon ground cinnamon*
> *½ teaspoon ground nutmeg*
> *3 cups water*
> *2 cups white sugar*
> *1 tsp vanilla extract*

Preheat oven to 400 degrees and butter a 9x13 inch pan. On a lightly floured surface, roll pastry into a large rectangle, about twenty-four by sixteen inches, and cut into six square pieces. Place an apple on each pastry square with the cored opening facing upward. Cut butter into eight pieces and place one piece of butter in the opening of each apple, reserving the remaining butter for sauce. Divide the brown sugar between apples, poking some inside each cored opening and the rest around the base of each apple, and sprinkle cinnamon and nutmeg over the apples.

With slightly wet fingertips, bring one corner of the pastry square up to the top of the apple, then bring the opposite corner to the top and press together. Bring up the two remaining corners and seal, then slightly pinch the dough at the sides to completely seal in the apple. Repeat with the remaining apples. Place in prepared baking dish.

In a saucepan, combine water, white sugar, vanilla extract, and reserved butter. Place over medium heat and bring to a boil in a large saucepan. Boil for five minutes, or until sugar is dissolved, and carefully pour over dumplings.

Bake in preheated oven for 50 to 60 minutes. To serve, place each apple dumpling in a bowl and spoon some sauce over the top.

SPICED PUMPKIN BUTTER
(with thanks to Chloe Shepard)

1 lb. sugar pumpkin or 15 oz. pureed pumpkin
½ cup apple cider
1 cup brown sugar
2 tbs maple syrup
½ tsp ground ginger
¼ tsp ground cloves
¼ tsp ground nutmeg
1 tsp ground cinnamon

If using fresh pumpkin, cut the pumpkin into pieces, removing seeds and stringy parts, and remove the stem and "butt." Place pumpkin, skin side down, on a baking sheet and bake at 325 degrees for about an hour. Let cool. Remove the skin and puree the pumpkin in a food processor, adding a small amount of water if needed.

Mix pumpkin and remaining ingredients together in a large saucepan. Bring mixture to a full boil over medium-high heat. Reduce heat and continue cooking ten to fifteen minutes or until thickened, stirring frequently. Remove from heat. When slightly cooled, spoon into clean jars and refrigerate.

ACKNOWLEDGMENTS

First, many thanks to my family, Eric, Abby, and Ian, not just for putting up with me, but for continuing to come up with creative ways to kill people. (You should see the looks we get in restaurants.) I also want to give a shout-out to Carol and Dave Swartz, Dorothy and Ed MacInerney, and Bethann and Beau Eccles for their years of continued support. Special thanks to the MacInerney Mystery Mavens (who help with all manner of things, from covers to concepts), particularly Mandy Young Kutz, Georgette Thaler, Rudi Lee, Olivia Leigh Blacke, Alicia Farage, Samantha Mann, Azanna Wishart, Priscilla Ormsby, and Chloe Shepard for their careful reading of the manuscript. What would I do without you??? Kim Killion, as usual, did an amazing job on the cover design, and Randy Ladenheim-Gil's sharp editorial eye helped keep me from embarrassing myself. I want to give a big shout-out to the folks at Trianon, particularly Chloe, Ashley, and Stephen, for keeping me motivated (i.e. caffeinated) and being such terrific company. Thanks also to John Carlton and Kaori Sakamoto for their generous technical advice (any errors are mine, not theirs), and to Jason Brenizer for being my faithful writing buddy and plot brainstormer. And finally, thank you to ALL of the wonderful readers who make Dewberry Farm possible, especially my fabulous Facebook community at www.facebook.com/karenmacinerney. You keep me going!

ABOUT THE AUTHOR

Karen is the housework-impaired, award-winning author of multiple mystery series, and her victims number well into the double digits. She lives in Austin, Texas with two sassy children, her husband, and a menagerie of animals, including twenty-three fish, two rabbits, and a rescue dog named Little Bit.

Feel free to visit Karen's web site at www.karenmacinerney.com, where you can download a free book and sign up to receive short stories, deleted scenes, recipes and other bonus material. You can also find her on Facebook at www.facebook.com/AuthorKarenMacInerney or www.facebook.com/karenmacinerney (she spends an inordinate amount of time there). You are more than welcome to friend her there—and remind her to get back to work on the next book!

CPSIA information can be obtained
at www.ICGtesting.com
Printed in the USA
BVHW042339210423
662863BV00014B/170

9 781976 029882